SICARIONAUTS

SICARIONAUTS

Saving the World! Yes Really

ANTHONY ACOSTA

Kennedy Media Group

CONTENTS

With Love For
Fabiola and Kennedy

With Deep Appreciation For

Will, Chewie, Oscar, Sonny, Carjack, Rommel
and Barry

...and a special mention:
Mrs. White, my 10th Grade English Teacher
who took extra time to let me know how much
I suck at writing. She forced me to up my
game, and now I still suck at writing, but now I
can do it much more eloquently.

CHAPTER 1

No Matter

Astronaut George Jones stared in amazement from the observation copula in the International space station at the spectacular unobstructed view of the brilliant stars. As he was awed by the scene, he produced a small digital recorder that he used to catalog his thoughts.

Taking a deep breath, he speaks into the device, "Staring out into the awesome and overwhelming vastness of space. Ignoring the beautiful blue sphere we call earth. These are the voyages of the great astronaut, the legendary Geo Jones! His quest? To find the mythic—"

"Geo! What the hell are you doing?!" Interrupted by his fellow astronaut Roy, he responds

"Ah, nothing, I was just—"

"C'mon now buddy. Time to git out of the Copula. We gotta get to the snowcone."

Glancing one last time at the beautiful vista outside, he exited the small module. He floated up, away from the impressive window array that always reminded him of that legendary ship from the famous space movie.

Feeling kind of jovial, he joins Roy Ross. Roy always seemed a little tall to be an astronaut, he thought, but the skinny payload specialist from Alabama was one of the best space-walking astronauts NASA had ever seen. As they make their way through the cramped science modules and through the connecting nodes on their way to the far end of the station, Roy remarks to him, "I think she's figured it out this time, She keeps talking about how Albert Einstein had it right, and that he would be proud."

"Really?" Geo responded, "I know we've been able to maintain the temperature near absolute zero; do you think she'll be able to create the particle and keep it stable?"

"I don't know, but we've got to get there. You know the protocol. You need to be ready to launch the snowcone if something does go wrong."

Roy always smirked when he said snowcone. It had a formal scientific name, the 'spacial **n**ano-**w**ave **c**ondensate **o**bservation **e**xperiment' which was SNWCOE, but Roy simplified it to SNOWCONE. Roy was someone who took very few things seriously, which is why this name always caused him to chuckle.

The apparatus had been attached to the ISS a few months earlier. It resembled a snowball with a cone protruding, pointy end out. Scientists had hoped to create a new state of matter. Something they called the 'fifth-state.' That's what they called it anyway; he knew that it was a smart way of avoiding the words 'dark-matter' which gave everyone chills. The bureaucrats would have pulled the funding if they knew that this science project was trying to produce dark matter.

Though he had to admit that he didn't know much about it, he did know it was a big deal in certain scientific circles. Regardless he thought, safety first. As astronauts on the ISS, their job was to execute scientific experiments which boiled down to following the instructions on the protocols for each experiment. In the case of this experiment, his job was to act as the safety officer. If the particle got out of control, it was his job to eject the cone away from the station and ensure that it explodes far away from any space objects, especially the earth.

As they arrived at the far end of the station, they passed through the last node and into the Fifth State Lab, or FSL as indicated by the small placard at the entrance. He loved coming to this Lab. While the rest of the station was cramped and hoses and supplies were covering almost all the surfaces, the FSL was more extensive and incredibly well organized. No cables and wires were visible as they were cleverly from view, behind white storage containers, which lined the walls evenly, creating a kind of zen other worldly feel.

Dr. Karen Nelson was impatiently waiting for them at the far end of the FSL. Her slender form quietly floated in the compartment as she was studying her notes. Her pale skin contrasted with her long black hair, which flowed wildly through the zero-g environment, momentarily making her appear like a phantom, or maybe a troll doll, although he was never sure which. She was a theoretical physicist by trade, and she spent most of her time at some university research lab. But her breakthrough in dark matter research made her the world's foremost expert on the 'fifth-state' of matter. She had been working at CERN when it shut down—She immediately picked up funding and resources to continue her project on the ISS. She was the one who was in charge of this experiment, which, she hoped, would allow them to create and observe the dark-matter within a stable field.

"C'mon guys," she scolded, "Don't make me wait. It will work this time."

Roy flashed a sarcastic smile.

"That's what She—"

"Don't say it. Roy," he responded quickly, not letting Roy finish his quip. His humor, while wildly inappropriate, was great for morale.

Roy looked back at him and shrugged his shoulders, "What?, I wasn't going to say anything" and flashed that knowing smile. Sure they joked around a lot; it was a side effect of being in such close quarters for an extended period. If anyone didn't have a sense of humor, they wouldn't last.

Karen didn't acknowledge the childish reply from Roy, although he secretly knew she enjoyed it. Another side effect of living in close quarters is that flirtations become welcome. "C'mon guys," she said, "We're standing on the shoulders of geniuses and peering into the great mysteries of the universe." Are you making childish jokes? Clearing his throat, Roy suddenly got serious. "No ma'am. My apologies, ma'am. Sometimes I find that humor is a great way to lighten any tension."

Karen nodded. "Ok, then. Let's proceed". She took the central position on the module facing the snowcone controls. Roy floated on one end as he monitored an array of displays showing the various energy readings from the experiment. Karen would operate the internal force emitters that were the heart of the experiment. Operate is a strong word. The system was run by a clever AI which did most of the work, but still needed an operator to activate and adjust the emitters. His task was to monitor the progress visually and be ready to eject if the need to abort arose. He needed to make sure the snowcone ejected in time. But also that it would clear the station and any other space objects.

"Initializing," she stated.

Proceeding to push several buttons on the panel, they could hear the deep sounds of generators engaging.

"Profile is nominal," Roy responded.

"Acknowledged," she replied. "Proceeding with quantum entanglement functions."

The sounds of whirring from the rapidly moving robotic arms manipulating unseen energy fields filled the chamber. The tension was thick, but the experiment appeared to be proceeding normally.

As the particles converged in the chamber, a small bluish-white light suddenly flashed into existence.

"We have condensates," Karen stated excitedly. "We need to hold them together in the quantum field!" She continued manipulating the mechanical arms. "How's the temperature holding?" She asked Roy.

"It's holding. We're at absolute-zero."

She was beaming. "It's stable! It's stable!" She shouted out excitedly. "YES! We did it!" "I was right!" now she was screaming with excitement.

The small pinhole light was no longer fluctuating. It was a steady glowing particle no more substantial than the tip of a needle, but it represented a quantum leap forward in our understanding of the universe.

"Guys, you're looking at the first stable dark matter ever to be created. YES! Nobel, here I come!" She shouted as her composure transformed from an accomplished scientist to an ambitious and excited little girl as she let her inner child take over. Roy, never one to miss a chance, turned to her with open arms, "Congratulations!" He said with a big smile. She was too excited to care about any ulterior motives and accepted the celebratory hug.

As they were busy celebrating, the tiny light started fluctuating.

"Uh, guys?" Geo responded. Instantly, the celebration cut short as Roy and Karen rushed back to their stations. "Roy, talk to me." She said as he examined the readouts. "We're losing the quantum lock; the field is destabilizing." He replied with seriousness. "I can hold it," Karen said as she concentrated on adjusting the robotic arms. As she did, the tiny light started growing. It was flashing waves of particles that didn't seem to care if they passed through solid matter. The waves were extending beyond the testing chamber. They had begun shining through the ISS's hull, not caring about solid barriers. It was as if they were present in an overlapping dimension, and the walls of that dimension were suddenly collapsing onto ours.

He had to call it. These effects were not usual, and the danger to the ISS was a lot more substantial than anyone had thought. "I have to abort!" Geo shouted in alarm, "Adjusting trajectory." He manipulated a small joystick that controlled the cone. He had to make sure they didn't eject it towards the earth. His augmented display showed him the locations of other satellites and celestial obstructions. He looked around with the joystick until he found an available window among the objects where he could safely launch the snowcone. "Got it!" he announced, "Ejecting!" pushing the red abort button, instantly launching the snowcone, and the dark-matter inside of it, away from the ISS at incredible speeds. Within seconds, it was hundreds of miles away. "Look away!" Roy shouted, and they all ducked and shut their eyes!

A split second later, a flash of pure white light shone brilliantly in space ten times brighter than the sun. The explosion had occurred across several dimensions, and the effect was awesome, no, it was profoundly visceral. Imagine looking directly at the sun and closing your eyes. Now, imagine that it's so bright that it doesn't care that you closed your eyes and just pierced through your eyelids and your body as if you were transparent.

That was the brightness of this flash. For a precious few seconds everyone on this hemisphere of the planet was enveloped in the brilliant white light which by all accounts looked like a second sun in the sky. It lasted approximately ten seconds before dying off into nothingness.

There was absolute silence in the module. There were no words. The three astronauts just stared at each other as their eyes readjusted from the blinding light back into the familiar reality. Checking themselves for injury, they realized that the light had come from another dimension, they had only experienced the brightness, and nothing more. Nobody appeared hurt.

"Um, you think anybody else saw that?" Roy asked, breaking the silence. He and Karen just stared back at him incredulously.

In the days, weeks, and months that followed, this event, which affected the entire eastern hemisphere of the planet, became known as "The Flashing." The device became known as "The Snowcone of death." Now it should be understood that nobody died from the event. Nevertheless, it coincided as the unfortunate acronym derived from the title of the paper Dr. Nelson published in the scientific journals. "**S**pacial **N**ano-wave **C**ondensate **O**bservation Experiment **of D**iluted Energy in Absolute Zero **Th**reshold"

CHAPTER 2

Port of Brownsville

Benicio lit his cigarette and paused for a moment to enjoy the first drag of his terrible habit. He had a lot of them, but he always felt embracing his demons allowed him to be honest about being a sicario. Sure, his skill set was smuggling, kidnapping, and yes, killing when necessary, but he was always honest about his trade. He thought too many Sicarios try to deny their vices and wrap themselves in false virtue. This led to them always trying to hide who they really were, but it never worked because the vices would surface as they always do, and they would be unable to control them, which would always lead to chaos and their downfall. He felt, if a person pretended to be something they were not, then that meant they were hiding their vices. If they hid their vices, then that meant they couldn't control them. You can't trust someone who can't control their darker side. You'll always get burned. *Yes,* he thought, *he needed his vices.*

He looked across the nearby dunes at the impressive Space Logistics complex's distant lights as he stood next to his old truck. Eyes glinting from under the brim of his black Stetson. He reached to his side to feel the handle of his prized possession, a custom-built .50 Calibre Desert Eagle, adorned with intricate designs throughout. It featured the word *MUERETE* (Die) engraved along the barrel. He liked it, not so much for the damage it could inflict, but because the mere sight of it would instill fear in those who saw it. He never really had a taste for killing, but brandishing this impressive tool was more than enough to get him what he wanted.

He watched the nearby complex as they completed another successful test of their pretty spaceship. The whole thing looked quite beautiful as it was set against the vast south Texas evening skies.

He remembered the first time he saw those boosters landing. It was during a smuggling run on nearby Boca Chica beach. Hiding among the dunes, his truck loaded with contraband. On that day, Space Logistics was conducting engine tests, and the local authorities had closed access to the beach. No one would be around, making it the perfect time for smuggling. Getting contraband from nearby Bagdad beach in Mexico to Boca Chica Beach on the US side was pretty easy. The low tide revealed a wide enough area to allow a truck to get through. Sure, he had to avoid the Border Patrol and their seismic sensors, however, the rockets would produce enough vibrations that CBP agents would turn off the hidden devices. Allowing him to sneak through.

Today he wasn't smuggling. Today he had been tasked with something far more dangerous. His employer, the cartel, had ambitions to expand its territory. They wanted to take control of the Port of Brownsville in which he now stood. This seaport, with its large distinct gantry cranes, was the largest deepwater shipping port in south Texas. An exciting place for commerce, especially if one was aware of the hidden underworld brewing with opportunity and danger. Its strategic location made it a lucrative black market that was currently controlled by a rival cartel.

Parked just inside the southern edge of the Port, Benicio turned his attention to his best friend, who was currently lounging in his truck bed. Malote was one of those people who was designed to stand out. His rough face and dead eyes stood in stark contrast to his really colorful silk shirt. Benicio thought he wore them to draw people's attention away from his face. He loved showing off his gold necklaces, especially the one large gold and diamond-covered Santa Muerte pendant. He was obsessed with Santa Muerte. He believed this talisman protected them from harm in all their exploits. He was clutching the lucky necklace in one hand as he watched the far off activity. "It's beautiful, isn't it?" his partner in crime asked without looking away from the distant lights.

"Yes, it is,"

"You know," he continued. "When I was a kid, I used to dream about becoming an astronaut."

"Yeah, I know. You're always telling me."

This was true. Benicio nodded. *Sometimes when Malote got started talking, there was no shutting him up. Especially when he was talking about space.*

"I have always wanted to be like Lance Armstrong... All cool, walking on the moon, looking back down on our tiny planet."

Flashing a confused look. "You mean Neil."

"What?"

"Neil Armstrong. Not Lance. Lance Armstrong was that one—"

"Whatever man, you know what I mean."

"Yeah, I do."

Before Malote could go any farther into his childhood dreams, the sounds of a scuffle interrupted the conversation. Turning their attention towards the dark alley behind them. The door to a nearby warehouse flew open. Two masked men stepped into the darkness as they dragged a person behind them. His head concealed under a hood, hands bound as he futilely fought against his abductors.

"They're back, and they have Tavo."

"Yup, time to work."

Malote gave the distant spaceport one last glance before leaping off the back of the truck. Opening the passenger side door, the men loaded the prisoner. They tossed him into the cab as if he was a bag of potatoes.

Benicio admonished them, "Take it easy, We can't bring him in injured."

Malote shoved the man over as he climbed in. The prisoner was pinned between both of them in the truck. As Malote closed the door, He handed two envelopes full of cash to the masked men. Taking their payment, they nodded and quickly vanished into the night.

"Can you imagine the look on el Gallo's face when he finds out we've got his kid." Malote wondered out loud.

Ignoring his friend for a moment, Benicio turns the key. The sound of the powerful engine coming to life gives away this seemingly old truck's secret. This is a custom-built off-road monster hidden underneath an old shell. They are called sleepers, and Benicio is exceptionally proud of this one. This baby delivers over 700 horsepower and is equipped with military-grade suspension, making her the perfect truck for the unique South Texas landscape. He strokes the dashboard and smiles for a moment, admiring her, as he heads towards the Port's exit.

"All in a day's work, my friend," he finally replies. "All in a day's work."

Acquisition in India

Miksa Amari smiles to himself as he allows himself to enjoy the crisp mountain breeze coming off the nearby Himalayas in this predawn hour. The wind caressed his face through the open window of the speeding SUV. It's a small pleasure, but it gives him a momentary break from the pain that consumed him. *She would have enjoyed the wind,* he thinks to himself, remembering the love of his life. She was taken so suddenly, so unfairly. *It's OK my love, They will soon pay,* he thinks to himself as if to bring some comfort to an unseen spirit. Squeezing his eyes shut to block out the terrible visions. It didn't help. War can be hell. Images of coalition soldiers invading and shooting indiscriminately through his small Syrian village flash through his mind. His love's eyes dimmed as she lay dying. Then the sudden blinding flash turned everything white. He could feel the helplessness from that moment. He was determined to have his revenge.

Opening his eyes, his resolve once again focuses on the task at hand. Looking over to his compatriot, a large and imposing soldier named Macchar, who is driving their SUV through the treacherous dark mountain road. He says, "Slow down, don't drive too close to them." He turns to check the distance between them and the tail-lights from the other two vehicles in their nefarious caravan. "We don't want to mess this up before our journey even begins."

He's been planning this revenge for months. He recalled reading the news about the discovery scientists had made of the new state of matter, the so-called fifth-state, which had the potential to release unimaginable amounts of energy. It was so dangerous that scientists were only able to create it in outer space. The first time they were successful, they couldn't control it. They ejected it from the space station. Where it released massive amounts of energy. It created a momentary flash of light so intense that for a moment, his village and the entire hemisphere were enveloped in blinding daylight for a few minutes. This was also the same moment his wife had been stolen from him. To Amari, this fifth-state matter was a sign from God. A mandate from above to avenge her death, and he would not fail. Gaining trust through successfully executing a large number of missions for the Assad forces, had given him the resources the need to carry out this daring mission. He'd recruited nine soldiers to execute his vision, the first part of which was the most daring heist anyone had ever attempted. These jihadists consisted of himself, his best friend Macchar, Jarah, an electronics guru, and six of the most well-trained mercenaries in the country.

The caravan rounded the mountain pass, the top of an enormous stone statue of Shiva came into view. This ancient stone deity rose several hundred feet over the overgrown foliage and demanded any onlooker's attention. Startled by her sudden presence, he could not escape her gaze, which pierced through his soul as if knowing his intentions. She appeared to be watching and following him. Her stone hands are frozen in the Abhaya mudra (A gesture of fearlessness, reassurance, and safety).

"Focus!"

He shouted at the distracted Macchar, who had also been mesmerized by Shiva. He quickly turned his attention back to the road ahead. "The entrance is approaching," Amari announced into the Communications earpiece, to the rest of the team. He'd studied and bribed his way to obtain all the information he could gather about the Indian Space Research Organization, otherwise known as the ISRO. Aware that they had built a facility in this valley at the base of the monolithic statue of Shiva. They had hidden it in plain sight among abandoned temples and enormous ancient statues that riddled this part of the country. Knowing that they were on the verge of launching their own state of the art rocketship on this day he thought to himself;

This is it, this is the day, the hour, the moment we will change the world!

The silence was broken as Macchar announced, "The gate," while nodding ahead. This was a man of few words. So when the imposing man spoke, it always surprised him. At the same time, a small burst of radio static-filled Amari's ear as his communications earbud sprung to life. "Manara Leader, this is group One. We are ready to proceed on your mark."

"Jarah. Jam the phones," he ordered his electronics wizard. Jarah was in the back seat typing away at his laptop. Immediately he pulled out a small black box with a large antenna and switched it on.

"Signals have been disabled," Jarah acknowledged.

Taking a deep breath, he commanded, "Breach the gate."

The trio of vehicles immediately veered off the main road. Speeding quickly down the small path which led to the facility, they switched on their super bright light bars as they closed in on the guarded front gate. The sentries startled by the fast-approaching vehicles and blinded by the sudden onslaught of painfully bright lights were frantically reaching for their weapons.

Macchar took this as his instruction as well. As the deadly caravan rammed through the gate, Macchar aimed the SUV directly for a guard who had managed to jump out of the way of the first two vehicles. Macchar made sure he solidly connected with the guard. His body spun off into the darkness with a loud *thump*. The unexpected impact caused him to glare at Macchar, "Really?"

"You said to go, so I go." Macchar shrugged.

He grinned a little at his overzealous driver. "OK then, let's go!" pointing ahead towards their goal. Almost instantly, security alarms announced their arrival. Aware of the activity sweeping through the facility, blaring sirens, distant yelling followed by quick bursts of gunfire. He closed his eyes as he refocused on the mission at hand.

"Entrance has been secured. Ready to proceed to the main building, Sir." a voice in his ear interrupted his thoughts.

Taking the position behind his team, they flanked him comfortably in a tight delta formation. They quickly ran to the doors of the main building. One of the men approached it, slapped a small shaped charge, and signaled the group to stand back.

A second later, a larger than expected explosion tore the doors open, knocking them off their hinges and flying into the facility's lobby. Amari smiled. He wanted to make a dramatic entrance, and this was dramatic.

Proceeding inside quickly, they took control of the lobby, which was large, white, and empty, except for a reception desk at the far end of the room. Almost immediately, security personnel flooded into the space to offer resistance. Knowing that the soldiers he had recruited had much more experience and superior training, he watched as they subdued the opposition. The quick battle lasted all of seven seconds. Emboldened by the ease of this victory. He was more confident than ever that he had assembled a well oiled, deadly machine. Advancing quickly through the building, the elite crew made their way to Launch Control.

Entering this vast, open room, Ansari couldn't help but notice the enormous clear windows that lined the front of the room. They must be at least thirty or forty feet high and really impressive in their own right. He couldn't help but note how this room felt more like a cathedral, and somehow demanded reverence. However, remarkable windows were quickly forgotten as his eyes opened wide with awe and wonder at what lay beyond.

He found himself gawking like a little kid at the scene that filled the view. Taking a moment to really enjoy the sight, he let his eyes wander over every detail of the beautiful futuristic transport that stood before him. The sleek white spacecraft was resting on her launchpad at the other end of this facility. She looked almost alive as she towered over the facility. Wisps of condensation can be seen escaping from barely perceptible vents along the length of the fuselage. The mist-like whirls seemed like phantoms through the air. Written on the side of the vessel, was her name. ISRO Chandra. They had named her after the lunar deity, 'Lord Chandra.'

The vessel looked like she was ready to shed the shackles that kept her on the ground. She seemed eager to escape the firmament and soar beyond the sky, piercing through the veil into space. She is a thing of unexplainable beauty, not just because of the hard work that went into her creation but also for what she meant for the future of the space industry. Well aware that while NASA and Space Logistics had promised leaps in the advancement of space exploration, the intensely secretive team at ISRO was actually delivering. They had experienced incredible success in space vehicle development he recalled from his research. All of that enormous potential was not lost on him. But it didn't matter as the majestic ship was simply a convenient ride to him—one which would take him closer to fulfilling his destiny of revenge.

Looking away from her, he turned his attention to assess this cathedral-like place. There were several levels of landings that overlooked the massive room, much like balconies. Launch control was occupied by unarmed scientists, lab techs, and researchers. Their dramatic intrusion had halted all activity in the room as his new-found hostages starred in fright at the armed invaders.

Silently but intensely, he stared down his prisoners, slowly studying everyone he made eye contact with, making sure they looked away first. This technique for establishing his dominance had served him well, and he derived some pleasure from doing it.

Once he was satisfied that he had successfully intimidated everyone here, he broke the silence. Commanding his men, "Group One. You're in charge of this room. Group Two, follow me."

The team immediately split. Group One consisted of three armed men who took up tactical positions around the room. Group Two consisted of three armed men but also Macchar, Jarah, and himself. Heading to the second level, he's aware of the need to launch the Chandra before the launch window passes. Scanning this level, he quickly notices the flight director huddling in a corner. As he starts walking in the frightened man's direction, he's suddenly interrupted as an angry older engineer who attempts to confront him.

"I don't know what the hell you think you're—"

BANG! Before the engineer could finish his sentence, he was struck by a bullet to the neck and dropped dead on the spot. Surprised by the sudden gunshot, he turned to look at his team. None of them appeared to have made a move.

"Who did that?"

One of his men slowly raised his hand like a schoolboy called out by his teacher.

"That was a nice shot. Good Job."

The man flashed a quick smile then returned his rigid pose.

Looking around, once again, to his now shocked audience. He suddenly relaxes his posture.

Greeting them as if they were long lost, acquaintances. "Hello. I just want to say that I'd really prefer no one else die here today," he said with a smile. "But, as you can see, My men won't hesitate to kill anyone who resists. So please, for your own safety, I'm simply asking that you listen and follow the commands given to you. Especially from that guy." Amari said as he pointed to the soldier who had just shot the engineer. "Do that, and no more blood will be spilled here today."

His attention was drawn to the large countdown clock on the far wall as he spoke. It read 15:07. *Still, plenty of time, assuming nothing went wrong,* he thought to himself.

Turning his attention back out through the large windows to gaze at the Chandra. He could once again feel her beckoning him. Without looking away, or even blinking, he spoke in a commanding tone.

"Who's in charge here?"

"That...that would be me," replied a man standing at the far end of the room as he stepped forward cautiously. He seemed somewhat fearful, but not for himself, but for the men in his charge.

Turning to measure the greying middle aged bureaucrat Amari asked."What is your name?"

"Tyson"

"Mr. Tyson. This facility is now under the control of the *Zalam Jihad*. No harm will come to you so long as you cooperate. Our goals are for the moment aligned. Just like you, we want your launch to go smoothly and successfully. We are simply here to make a change to your passenger manifest."

Glancing once again at the launch clock. "Don't do anything reckless. Make sure everything goes as planned. Do you understand?"

"I... I... I do, but... what can you possibly—"

Slap!

Tyson was clearly surprised by the quick unexpected assault.

"No. No questions." Amari scolded Tyson. He produced a small phone from his pocket.

"Here," handing the phone to Tyson,

"Record me."

Tyson took the phone with his trembling hands, managed to find the camera, and started to record. "Recording," he stated in a nervous voice.

Amari stood straight, he wanted to appear regal and confident. He spoke in a clear voice.

"For far too long, the world's superpowers have looked upon our people like we are cockroaches. A pest to be stomped on until exterminated. You have never given a second thought to our goal. All we want is to realize our beautiful dream of living a peaceful existence. In this existence, we will finally be rid of all of the infidels and those with dissenting opinions. You have never taken us seriously. Just because you believe differently from us, you think our desires or goals are not valid! If we do not think like *you*, then surely we must be wrong.

"Well, no longer will the Americans or the Russians or anyone else ever look down on us again. Allah has given us a great gift. Our quest to find peace and respect drives us to this, our greatest achievement! We will journey to the skies above the skies. It will be the Zalam Jihad who will take control of the International Space Station. We will take control of the fifth-state of matter, aim it over our enemies, and in a single moment, bathe the hemisphere in God's holy light. In a single moment, we will decimate the west.

You will then submit to us and recognize our authority! From this moment on, every man, woman, or child will tremble upon hearing our name! What is left of the world will bow down to the Zalam Jihad!"

Amari motioned to Tyson to quit recording. Tyson complied and handed the phone to Amari with trembling hands.

Amari spoke, "The launch is to proceed as planned. If anything goes wrong, my men will execute everyone here... and when they are done, they will locate your families and kill your children. Do you understand?"

Tyson nodded. He looked around with wide eyes, perhaps realizing, for the first time, just how severe this situation had become. "Once we launch, your phone service will be restored. Release this video to all media outlets. We WANT the world to know what is coming."

Amari glanced at the countdown clock, which now read 11:36.

"Mr. Vowles, you have eleven minutes to direct us to the flight-ready room and get us on that rocket."

"What? There's ...that's not nearly enough time."

"For your sake, I hope it is," he admonished the man. Feeling the need to emphasize his threat, "If I am not on the Chandra when it launches, you will all die. And then your children and families. Look into my eyes. Do you not believe me?"

"I do... I.. I believe you."

"Good," Amari said, glancing out at the waiting craft. "Make it happen."

Tyson nodded, looking a little pale and definitely terrified.

"This way."

He led Amari and his men to the astronaut prep area.

As he did so, Amari thought, *these are the first steps to a new future, a new reality*. He smiled.

CHAPTER 3

One small Favor

Garrett Parker stared at his watch. It was precisely 7:15pm central time in Brownsville, Texas, or more accurately, Boca Chica Beach, Texas. Garrett enjoyed the view from his large luxurious office perched on a tower ten stories above the Space Logistics Complex. Even at this height, he could feel the deep vibrations as a rocket touched down outside on the nearby launchpad. Another successful mission, he thought to himself. Pleased with the progress the company is making towards maintaining a reliable pipeline into space. He's feeling more confident than ever, he'll succeed in dominating the space-faring future.

He enjoyed watching all the activity from his perch as several crew members ran out to the spacecraft, some in little golf carts, and others on foot. He'd watched the rocket take off and land a dozen times now, and he never got tired of it. In fact, a smile touched his face, and his chest swelled with pride. He'd always gotten a little misty-eyed when after the Pegasus rocket made a successful excursion, and this time was no different.

At the age of forty-eight, Garrett was the Billionaire CEO and President of Space Logistics Corporation. He held an eighty-five percent stake in the thriving company and had enjoyed the benefits of that wealth immensely.

But truth be told, Garret was not in it for the money, though. In fact, he wasn't even sure how much *he* was worth; he'd stopped keeping track after making the first billion. No, his vision was to transform humankind into a multi-planetary species. Sure, everyone thought he was crazy. They told him he was dreaming too big. But after making so many innovations and revolutionizing so many industries, they stopped calling him crazy. Instead, they started referring to him as a visionary.

Sipping an espresso he turned to watch one of the many TVs that lined the wall of his spacious office. One of his secret vices was reveling in what the public thought of Space Logistics. He couldn't wait to watch the report about the latest mission to deliver a new version of the 'fifth-state' experiment to the ISS would be on the news. He secretly relished in seeing the reports. The media was kind to his company. This was part of the reason he was given the contract to deliver the controversial snowcone. He would check in on social media and news sites—as he always liked to watch how the world reacted to his work.

Muting the screen, he watched as a reporter interviewed someone on Wall Street. Boring. Swiveling back around in his chair to admire his Pegasus, he settled in. However, before he could enjoy another sip from his espresso, his phone rang. A very select few had access to his private line: The Pegasus pilots, his wife, and a couple of VIPs in Washington. He answered the phone.

"Garrett here, speak," he said. He prided himself on his efficiency, and that greeting fit his personality well, plus he thought it was amusing.

A very flat and expressionless female voice responded. "Mr. Garrett, please hold for the President of the United States."

Although taken aback, he did enjoy the excitement that came with receiving a call from the President. He'd spoken with him on a few occasions. One of which had been over drinks in the White House Rose Garden with other movers and shakers in the space travel industry. He recalled being thrilled that the President and he shared so many world views. Still, it was thrilling to hear the voice on the other end of the line.

"Garrett Parker, Hello, How are you?"

Garrett smirked a little; he could never get over hearing the President of the United States referring to him by name. "I'm good, Mr. President. Are you calling about the latest flight? If so, I'm happy to report that all went well. The payload was delivered and installed, and I think we might be on track to—"

"I'm sorry to interrupt," The President said hastily. "That's not why I'm calling. Listen, Garrett... I need to ask you for a favor."

"Of course," Garrett said. In his mind, he assumed it would be a trip somewhere overseas—either Japan or India, where other space programs were being run. Maybe a consortium to host. He'd never spoken on behalf of the President before and was rather proud to think this might be the case now.

"The information I'm about to give you is top secret and must not go beyond this phone call, Garrett. Am I understood?"

"Yes, of course." Dreams of speaking on behalf of the President were shot down immediately. And was that *anxiety* he heard in the President's voice?

"What is it, sir?"

"Something has happened. Normally, the Space Force would take care of it, but this has happened much sooner than expected. We are finding ourselves inadequately prepared at the moment." There was a pause.

Space Force was the name for the new military branch that was tasked with monitoring and policing space operations. As a matter of fact, the snowcone he had just delivered was part of the reason the Space Force was approved. They were working in secret, building military rockets for operations in space, with an eventual (and likely) goal of setting a permanent base on the moon by 2024. Garrett had bid on these projects, but they were yet to be approved.

"Compromised *how*, sir?"

"A group of terrorists known as the Zalam Jihad has taken control of an ISRO research facility in India. They managed to hijack a rocket and have threatened to take control of the snowcone on the ISS and aim it at the continental United States. They launched twenty minutes ago."

"How is that even possible?" Garrett said. "The base in India... We know about their research. They're not anywhere near launching a rocket. Terrorists couldn't pilot a spaceship? Could they?"

"I'm aware of that. But regardless of what we think we know, we are sure those sons-a-bitches have done it. Intelligence is telling me that the ISRO rocket will reach the Space Station in a little under four hours."

Garrett nearly dropped his espresso. What he was hearing was impossible. To hijack the base in India was one thing...but for terrorists to self-launch into orbit was the stuff of nightmares.

"This is disastrous. How can I help?"

"I have a team headed your way from Corpus Christi. Their helos will be landing at your location in a few minutes. I need you to get them on the Pegasus and up to the ISS STAT."

"What sort of team? And... wait... *what?*"

"Son, more things are going on in the Space Force than anyone is aware of, even you. Just think of this as a kind of Space Force Seal Team. These are combat-trained astronauts. Just get them to the ISS before the terrorists get there."

"Sir, the Pegasus just landed and—"

"That's good. The engines are already warm then. You can skip a few steps and get her ready to go again."

"Sir, that's extremely dangerous. There's system diagnostics that need to be run, inspections, fuel, and oxygen checks—"

"No time. Garrett... I don't need to tell you that this is a huge opportunity for you and for Space Logistics. Just get the thing back in space as soon as possible."

"Sir, that's not exactly how it works. We can't—"

"How soon can you launch again?"

"Maybe an hour."

"Make it forty-five minutes," the President demanded. "For God's sake, son. They've already got twenty minutes on us."

"Yes sir," Garret replied, his heart thumping in his chest. Were they really talking about this? It was absolute lunacy.

"Don't let me down on this, Garrett. We have to do everything in our power to stop those terrorists. They must not get on board the space station. There's no telling what would happen if the snowcone is launched towards the planet. The fate of the world is in your hands."

"Yes, sir."

"Godspeed, Garrett."

The line went dead.

Garret looked back out to the window, unaware that his jaw was still open. *No pressure*, he thought. A quick curse later, he snapped back into action, picking up the handset to contact the flight director in the master control room.

"We're launching again right now. Keep the pilots on board. Refuel the Pegasus." he commanded.

"What? Sir, but we've already started—"

"Stop. No excuses. Fire everything back up. We're launching again. Top Secret Mission."

Even saying it, he had trouble believing it. The thought that terrorists were now part of the mix in the space race chilled him to the bone.

"Yes, Sir," the flight director responded, clearly confused. "How soon?"

"I need the Pegasus ready to launch in less than forty-five minutes.."

"Sir...are you n—?"

This time it was Garrett that ended the call. He looked out through the window to the massive and gleaming marvel he'd built. He knew the Pegasus was up to the task. Still, this mission had to succeed. The fate of the world was in his hands. *Besides*, he thought, *they'd done this so many times before, what could go wrong?*

CHAPTER 4

The Dunes

Benicio was very proud of his truck. For the casual onlooker, it looked like a 90's F150 covered in tarnish with an old brush guard and a lift kit. The typical working farm vehicle commonly found in South Texas. However, he had made sure that this appearance was intentional. He'd added armor plating beneath the old exterior and had replaced the stock engine with a 700 hp beast. He'd also acquired military-grade axles for added support. To keep the whole thing together, it had roll bars inside the cab. He smiled, proud of his baby as the engine rumbled along, deep and powerful.

Knowing that his truck was often underestimated was one of his strengths. No one was ever alarmed when he showed up. Everybody would just assume that he was part of the blue-collar workforce. Yes, he thought, this is my cloaking device. The vehicle gave him a considerable advantage when conducting his treacherous business. As a smuggler, or in this case, a kidnapper, he needed to be inconspicuous.

As Benicio was thinking about the truck and how they were escaping the Port, the silence was broken as their prisoner started acting up. He was trying to get out of his restraints.

Suddenly, Malote slapped Tavo hard. "Te callas el pinche osico o te lo rompo" Malote threatened their prisoner. He sounded ruthless, although there was a smirk on his face. "Ya calmate, pinche pendejo!" Their prisoner settled down. Malote looked back at him and quietly grinned while giving him a thumbs up. It wasn't exactly professional, but Benicio couldn't help but smile.

His smuggling had brought him to this place several times a week. Although many didn't know him personally, the distinct deep sound of his truck's powerful engine was a dead giveaway that he was approaching. That's why, when he and Malote arrived at the security gates at the port entrance, no one bothered to stop them. The two guards simply nodded knowingly at the truck as it passed. If they noticed the man bound and hooded sitting between them, they apparently did not care. One of the guards did not even look up from his phone as he numbly scrolled through his social feed.

Benicio guided the truck out of the Port and turned down the small connecting road that took them out to State Highway 4 a few hundred yards away. The evening sky was getting dark, and the street lights skirting the highway ahead were turning on. He loved this time of day. It made him feel like he was coming to life. Nighttime was his playground, and he knew her well.

Malote was playing around with the radio. He loved listening to metal. He tuned in to the local rock station, they had just started playing Black Betty, one of Malote's favorite hits.

"Leave it there. Awesome," Benicio said, as he tapped on the steering wheel to the deep beats waiting for the words to start. They were pumped. They started lip syncing as the lyrics came over the speakers when suddenly, the back window of his truck shattered. There was no splintering or cracking, just an explosion of glass that came flying through the cab.

The shocked hooded man between them let out a yell. Malote ducked turned to look behind them, letting out a quick "fuck!". Focusing on the road, he was going to ask his friend what he could see behind them, but the unmistakable sound of gunfire gave him the answer.

Trying to remain calm was impossible. Benicio and Malote were already pumped from the loud music, and the gunfire had triggered a sudden, more amplified adrenaline rush. Of course, this was not the first time he had been shot at, and he was pretty sure it wouldn't be the last time.

Malote had his gun out, he was attempting to identify their attackers. "Looks like El Gallo's men!" he gasped as he ducked to avoid any stray rounds. "I guess they didn't like us kidnapping his son." He said through a nervous laugh. He glanced at Malote, letting him know that his sarcastic comment had been received. Confident in his truck, he knew that their pursuers were already too late. Had they accosted them before leaving the Port, things might have gone sideways. But now, with the highway less than half a mile away, he knew he could escape them.

The gunfire continued to ring out around them. Tavo, who couldn't do anything due to the restraints, was relegated to angrily striking back verbally. "You morons forget who my father is?" Tavo screamed from beneath the hood. "Our men will gut you like the bottom-feeding scumbag pendejos that you are. You stupid cabrones!"

Malote responded by pistol-whipping Tavo on the side of his head. "Ya, cayate! We'll kill you right here and now!" Malote pistol whipped him again "Calmate, Malote!" Benicio remarked. "Don't hurt him too much!"

"Are you kidding me? Esos idiotas are putting holes in your truck! They don't care si lo matan, so why should we?"

It wasn't precisely sound logic, that was for sure. But Benicio was too focused on driving to argue with his friend. He was pushing the engine to gain speed—seventy-five to eighty, eighty-five to ninety. Behind them, their pursuers were keeping up. *Did they have new trucks,* he thought, *shit, they might catch us.* Even if he *did* make it to the highway before they overtook him, he wasn't so sure it would matter.

Got to lose them, he thought. *It was time to test his truck off-road. Let's see if all those mods pay off.* The highway lay straight ahead, and there were only sand dunes on either side—

His thoughts were broken apart by another deep boom. This one was not glass, not metal... in fact, it didn't sound like it came from anything on his truck. No, this time, the blast came from elsewhere in the night.

To the east, the horizon lit up. The glow came from the direction of the spaceport.

The rocket, he thought. *Is it lifting off again?...*

He didn't know. All he knew was that there was a convenient distraction over there, something that might help them getaway.

Aw hell, he thought as he took a sharp left turn. The truck skidded off of the road, struck the shallow ditch, and then went barreling through the air onto the sand.

"What the hell?!" Malote said. But then he smiled as he understood what his friend was up to.

Benicio shifted the truck into four-wheel drive mode. The pitch on the motor changed as the tires churned over the sand. He could hear the screeching of tires behind him as El Gallo's men tried to follow. But he knew it would not matter. Even if they managed to chase them through the dunes, their newer and more expensive vehicles were not built for racing off-road.

Proof of this came seconds later as the sounds of machine-gun fire tapered off to nothing more than a series of annoying little pops. The headlights of the pursuing vehicles grew smaller and smaller until they were nothing more than tiny specks in the distance. They might still be giving chase, but it was not close at all now.

"Good thinking," Malote stated. He glanced at Malote to acknowledge, but he was not looking at him, he was looking ahead. The facility was much closer than they realized, and the rocket got larger as they quickly closed the distance. The brightness from the lights illuminating the launch pad was drawing them in like moths to a flame. He could see a glow emanating from her rocket engines. He thought for a second that she might very well be moments away from another launch.

"No way, she just landed," he thought out loud as he continued to navigate the unpredictable dunes. The bumps were hard as they careened haphazardly through the rough spots. The hard music continued to blare and it perpetuated his aggression. Feeling reckless, he justified his destructive driving as a way to keep away from El Gallo's men. Secretly, he was just happy to see the full potential of his truck on full display. Yes, this is what he lived for.

Smoke was starting to billow out from under the hood. "I think they hit the engine!" He shouted, "We're not gonna last much longer."

That decides it then, Benicio thought. *Nowhere to go now other than towards that rocket.*

CHAPTER 5

Launch Pad

Garrett glanced at the countdown clock on his office wall. It was T minus 3:11 to launch. Still uneasy with the Pegasus going back up so soon after returning, but he knew she could do it. After all, one of the Pegasus project goals was to figure out ways to make rockets a viable form of transportation, able to come and go with the airplane's ease and efficiency. This mission would definitely test this.

Garrett thought about the pilots. They were two good men and great pilots. The only thing that really worried him was that he knew that they relied on a plan. These pilots' philosophy was to never do anything without a plan. In fact, they liked having a back plan for their initial plan. However, they were about to re-launch at a moment's notice. Because of the secret and urgent nature of this mission, they had only a minimal briefing on why they were launching again. Much information had been kept from them, which definitely put them outside of their comfort zone. Yes, he thought, This unusual mission was definitely going to be tough on them. "They'll be fine." He said out loud to no one in particular.

Looking out at the Pegasus, her body vibrating ever so slightly as her engines were primed. They were finalizing the preparations as she prepared to launch. The countdown clock read 3:01 when the intercom buzzed to life. "Sir! check your cameras!" It was the panicking voice of the flight director.

"I have it up on my screen," Garrett answered. "I don't see anything, It all looks normal."

"Not the launch pad, sir. The perimeter fence."

"The helicopters from Corpus Christi should be arriving now," Garrett replied. He had not told anyone about the contents of his call with the President. But he *had* informed them that there were going to be new VIP passengers on this next launch who were arriving by helicopter.

"Not the helicopters, sir. Just...just *look.*"

"What is it?"

But even as he asked, he had started scanning the perimeter cameras. Focusing on one of the feeds, his blood grew cold. *What is that?* He thought to himself as he watched an anomalous object closing in... Was it coming from the dunes?

The object on the screen couldn't be identified, they were definitely bouncing lights headed their way. Judging from their erratic behavior, the lights appeared to be out of control on the dunes. He was alarmed, for a second, he thought to himself, Even if we had a plan, we didn't have one for this. Even as this thought crossed his mind, He watched confused as the object had launched through the air and smashed over the perimeter fence. The screens turned white as, what looked like an explosion, filled the feed in front of his' horrified face.

What Garrett Parker saw as a plume of fire was, in fact, Benicio's truck. He had witnessed the moment Benicio's vehicle went airborne over a sand dune. Watching it fly over the perimeter fence and the spectacular crash on the tarmac. Holding his breath as he watched the wreckage come to rest just a few feet from the Pegasus.

As Garrett wrapped his mind around the events on his cameras. *No way this was real*. For a second, he thought, they're punking me. This is a terrible practical joke. Glancing around for hidden cameras, it dawned on him that this was no joke.

CHAPTER 6

Change of plan

Benicio sat motionless, still holding on to the steering wheel with a death grip. His mind was processing in disbelief what had just happened. For a second, he thought, what if I just died and now I'm a ghost stuck forever in this place. As the haze started lifting from his mind, he wasn't sure if he was elated or terrified at his predicament. Focusing on his hands, still gripping the wheel, he carefully wiggled a finger off the steering wheel, then another. Everything started coming back to him.

The fence had appeared out of nowhere, and by the time he had seen it, it was too late to stop. Recalling that he had come up with a simple plan to get around it, well, more like a plan to get over it. How simple that plan seemed. He recalled intentionally steering into one of the more towering dunes which lined the perimeter. For one naïve moment, as the truck was airborne, He thought they might clear the fence. He was sure they were *that* high off the ground.

Of course, that's not happened. Instead, what happened was, as the truck was airborne, the front end dipped enough to clip the top of the fence. It flipped over the barrier, sending the truck tumbling end-over-end, transforming it into a fiery ball of metal, oil, and gasoline. The wreck that used to be his prized truck was destroyed. It was an oversized crushed soda can which was emitting sparks, smoke, and was possibly on fire.

Thank God I installed that roll cage, he thought, *We'd be dead for sure.* After a few seconds, the trio of men inside that roll cage all screamed simultaneously.

"What the fuck!?" Tavo yelled.

Benicio ignored him as he climbed out of the driver's side window. Dusting himself off while examining the remains of his truck. Malote was doing his best to open the passenger side door. It had been severely compacted, so it did not budge. Giving up on it, Malote climbed out through what used to be the front windshield, dragging Tavo along as he emerged.

"You okay?" Malote asked as they quietly stood, staring at the wreck some fifteen feet away.

"I'm fine, guys. Thanks for asking," responded Tavo, still wearing the hood as he stood between them.

Slapping him on the back of the head, Malote retorted, "Not you pendejo, shut the fuck up." They stood in silence.

"Yeah," Benicio responded with a little bit of sadness in his voice. "I think my truck is dead," he stated. The three men stood there as if paying their respects to the destroyed transport. Suddenly, there was an explosion. A huge fireball went up out of the wreck, pushing them all backward. Looking around, the roar from the fiery wreck made it hard to hear. "We have to get away from here...somehow. I don't think El Gallo's men have given up." Malote screamed over the blaze.

Benicio looked around as the absolute absurdity of their situation dawned on him. He had successfully navigated through the dunes. Although he intended to get close to the complex, he wasn't planning on actually crashing into it. He was just trying to lose his pursuers. But now, this is where he was.

They had quite literally crash-landed onto the launchpad at Space Logistics. Not precisely the getaway he had imagined. The spacecraft he and Malote had admired from a distance less than half an hour ago now sat about fifty yards away from them. Exhaust and some sort of heavy chemical smell filled the air. He could feel the low rumbling of the rocket's priming engines in his bones.

"Ideas?" he asked Malote.

Malote shrugged, not knowing what to say.

Tavo, through his hood, suddenly shouted. "You two are the worst kidnappers ever! You're completely out of control, I ought to have—" Pow!, Malote punched him. "Hey man, shut the fuck up!"

Malote spoke up, "Security will be here any minute. So will El Gallo's men. And I don't know if—"

A new sound suddenly caught their attention. He thought he knew what it might be, but the constant hum of the rocket's engines made it hard to tell. Scanning the sky, sure enough, there were two black helicopters headed their way. They were already making their descent right next to them.

"You think those are for us?" Malote asked.

"Let's not find out!" replying over the noise. Thinking *No way, someone could have gotten those things over here so quickly...even if someone in the complex saw us out in the dunes. But, shit, they are right here, so they must be here for us.*

More alarms went off; these were piercing through his skull, interrupting his thoughts. *Alarms, security guards, Gallo's men, probably the police, and now these black helicopters,* Benicio thought. *Not sure I've ever had quite such a collection of people chasing me before.*

He could feel the panic starting to creep in. This was a familiar sensation as it was part and parcel of their profession, but it was still unpleasant. He usually managed to wrangle it away. But this insane convergence of events was almost too much for him. He had to keep the panic at bay.

"Benicio, Look!" Malote shouted.

Turning quickly, he watched as their prisoner had started to make a run for it. The hooded Tavo looked ridiculous as he was darting left and right at imaginary pursuers. His hood didn't let him see anything, but he was moving as fast as he could, not knowing where he was going. "Stupid," Malote commented as they just stood there for a moment watching the idiotic spectacle.

As they rushed to collect the blind "escaping" prisoner. They realized that he was, either intentionally or accidentally, headed towards a tiny building at the foot of the rocket. It wasn't exactly a building, it resembled some kind of smooth shipping container, although it was much smaller. *Was it attached to the gantry next to the rocket?* Benicio thought as the trio ran toward it. It was the only viable shelter anywhere nearby...not counting the rocket itself. For a second, he chuckled a bit, an image of them climbing aboard a rocket and blasting away to getaway flashed in his head.

Knowing that entering that small structure may only lead to being trapped, he ran there anyway. For now, at least, it was their only option. Supposing that if it came down to it, they'd just fight it out like Butch Cassidy and the Sundance Kid. Remembering that they would need weapons, he quickly felt for the pistol at his hip, the moment his hand touched it, he felt a sliver of comfort and confidence.

Glancing behind him, he couldn't believe the scene. There were security personnel coming towards them from all directions. Alarms blaring, lights flashing, he watched as several armed soldiers emerged from the helicopters. As if that wasn't enough, his eyes caught sight of the faint glow from El Gallo's men closing in. Their headlights were bobbing up and down as they bounced through the dunes towards them.

This is definitely nuts, he thought. He wasn't scared, but the little voice in his head that he kept ignoring was screaming in a panic as they reached the tiny shelter. Tavo reached the shelter first, Thud! As he slammed his head on the door while running at full speed. The impact knocked him on his back. Malote caught up to Tavo and immediately helped him back up as he lay into him with who knows how many threats and curses.

Approaching the structure, he noted that it was a bit larger than it first appeared. While there was a door, there was no door handle. However, there was a small black box next to the door, with a display, labeled: *'Open.'*

Benicio figured there was no harm in trying their luck. He reached out and tapped the screen. It lit up as the doors slid open. The screen now reads: *'Launch 1:44'.* This caused him to stop for a second and watch as the timer continued to count down. He paused for a moment and cocked his head to one side, trying to understand what that timer could mean.

As he hesitated, the armed men from the helicopters had made their way onto the tarmac. There were eight in all, three of whom were dressed in weird spacesuits, which made them resemble the stormtroopers from that famous movie.

"Hold it right there, or we will fire!" one the men shouted as he started to aim his weapon. They were really well-armed. The aggressive nature of their tone told him that they were going to open fire anyway. This was a bad situation.

"Fuck that!" Malote yelled. His anger and, perhaps, the tension of the moment, caught up with him. He ran through the open door, and, true to their word, the men opened fire. Two men shot, but Malote had already retreated into the structure dragging Tavo with him. As the gunfire came down all around them, Malote smashed the red button inside the structure, instantly slamming the doors shut. One second slower, and one of the shots would have hit him in the head.

"What the hell?" he yelled at his friend.

"Sorry," Malote said. "I thought I saw El Gallo's men getting close, and then those other pendejos started shooting at us—"

He did not finish his sentence before they heard someone shouting at them to come out. They also noted a second voice that appeared to be, not yelling at them, but at the soldiers demanding that they hold their fire or damage the lift.

Lift? Benicio thought. *What the hell?*

Up until now, the room they had stumbled into was dark except for a small illuminated digital display. The room suddenly brightened with a soft bluish-white glow from unseen lights. They looked around at this small empty room, which felt very white and very clean. The small display on the wall next to the door summoned their attention.

"What the hell kind of place is this?" Malote asked.

As if in response, the structure seemed to shudder a little and then, though it was impossible to tell for sure, felt as if they were being lifted. Thinking of where the structure was in relation to the rocket and recalled the countdown on the digital screen.

"Shit," he said.

"What?" Malote asked.

"It's an elevator. And we're going up."

"Up? Up to *what?*"

He knew the answer, but could not bring himself to say it. It was too crazy. It made no sense. How in God's holy name had they gotten themselves into this mess? He felt his nerves starting to overwhelm him and could feel his heart pounding. Suddenly, the room stopped moving upwards, and now they could feel it turning sideways. They could hear the hydraulics as the elevator came to rest in place. What they had thought was the back wall of the room suddenly opened on its own. It revealed a secondary door. This one was smooth and had almost invisible seams along its outline. It reminded Benicio of what he might see as the side of an airliner as he was boarding. Except, he knew this was no airplane. Right away, the seams appeared to push outward, and then suddenly, the door slid open.

As they were finding themselves out of options, they cautiously crept through the passageway. "What the..." He started to say. Knowing what he was looking at, but he really didn't want to accept it. Somehow, he knew they were now inside the cargo hold of the Pegasus.

CHAPTER 7

No no no!

Garrett Parker thought he was going to be sick as he watched the events unfolding on his screens. He thought back to when he was feeling pretty good about the future. Recalling just a few minutes ago, the President was asking him to facilitate a top-secret mission of great importance to save the world. He had been excited at the prospect and was confident that he'd succeed. It was such a highlight for him. Now, just forty minutes later, it had all collapsed into chaos. These new developments were threatening not only his company, but space force, and possibly the fate of the world.

A couple of minutes earlier, something that looked a lot like an old pick-up truck had come rocketing through the perimeter fence. It had wrecked next to the Pegasus and exploded. He watched it all happen, dumbstruck. How could this happen at his facility? How could this happen to him?

Then it hit him. It was a mistake to disable the safety protocols. He didn't have a choice, did he? This was the only way to get the military to the ISS in time. No, they had done the right thing. Struggling to find some kind of justification for the chaos happening outside. How could these intruders know precisely when to intercept the mission? Was it a mistake? Wait, Maybe they too are terrorists? Could this be what happened in India? He had a million questions running through his head. None of them quenched his stress. "Get it together, Garrett!" He told himself.

Maybe the intruders won't know what they're doing. Perhaps his crew could still fix the situation. It would take a miracle to save the mission. Oh, God.

For the first time in a long time, he felt utterly helpless. The stakes couldn't be higher, and the timing of these intruders couldn't have been worse. His engineers had calculated the emergency launch to the second so they could make the launch window. It was going to be tight as the launch window only lasted a few seconds. If they didn't make it in this one, the next launch window would be too late. They had calculated that there was just enough time for the incoming space force team to board the Pegasus and launch immediately.

No one could have foreseen that there may be party crashers. Much less, that the party crashers would intercept the same lift. As if this wasn't crazy enough, the intruders appeared to have brought their own hostage, as they were seen hauling a third man with them, his head covered and his hands bound.

Garrett could feel his blood pressure shooting up as he realized that he may have inadvertently facilitated a kidnapping. These events had put his prized project in peril. Oh, he had a sudden realization, The fate of the world was in danger too. Accommodating the Space Force, and having that effort sabotaged, was going to cost him dearly.

He looked away from the massive window in his office for only a moment, long enough to go to the door and scream out to the rest of the team. "Where the fuck is security?"

"On the launchpad, sir!" someone responded. "The Space Force is there along with our team. They are trying to access the lift."

"Oh my God," Garrett muttered. He was thinking, though, that even *if they do manage to get on board the Pegasus, they were still facing a possible hostage situation. "We're definitely going to miss the launch window," he uttered out loud. "The Space Force won't make it to the space station, and terrorists are going to do who knows what."*

He wondered for a second if something like this is what had happened in India.—if his Pegasus was being hijacked in the same way. *No, No way.* He muttered to himself, "The way these men were running towards the Pegasus looked more like they were running from something, not running to something. They had to be there by accident—"

"Mr. Parker?"

His intercom lit up. The voice was accompanied by the familiar crackling static that came only from the Pegasus' VHF communications. The Astronaut, Mike Fosum, a forty-seven-year-old aeronautics specialist and veteran of the NASA space program, and one of his most dependable and reliable pilots.

Garrett rushed to the phone and pressed the button to respond.

"Mike, hey. Give me some good—"

"We have confirmation that the elevator is coming up," Mike inadvertently interrupted. "Confirming this is the special cargo you want delivered to—"

"No, No No!" Calming himself down, he composed himself long enough to continue, "There's been a situation." Now it was Garrett who interrupted. "We need to scrub the launch."

"What? What's happening?"

"I don't know. Possible hijacking. Definitely party crashers. Do what they ask, but get them off the Pegasus as soon as possible."

"Sir, we're set to launch in one minute, or we'll miss the launch window."

"I know that Mike! just kill the launch! We'll get this sorted by the next launch window."

But that was it. There was nothing else Garrett could do. The elevators would retract in a few seconds. Even if the crew members could convince the intruders to get out, the delay would cost them dearly. The space force team wouldn't be able to reach the space station in time. There was nothing he or his billions of dollars or all of the Space Logistics corporation could do about it.

Garrett knew it was too late. He was aware that the elevator would power down before for the launch. When the Space Logistics team disabled the safety protocols, they also disabled the override for this function. The elevator would be useless. He was useless. It only took a few seconds to realize that all that power he had and there was nothing he could do about this.

He looked out his window. He could see the agitated Space Force team trying to override the locked-down elevator. He knew this was a doomed effort. He exhaled slowly. He then uttered the only word he could think of, to sum up, the current situation.

"Fuck."

CHAPTER 8

Lift off

"One minute to launch." A seemingly pleasant but artificial female voice was speaking through an unseen intercom.

"Launch?" Malote asked.

"Launch?" Tavo echoed from under his hood, his voice in a shrill sort of squeak.

Feeling trapped and honestly a little panicky, Benicio turned around and pounded on the Pegasus' Cardo door he had just come through. He could only see a single button near the door. He felt hope as he pushed it, assuming it would open the door. Instead, his hope was crushed by a harsh buzzing noise that sounded instead. He hit it again and again, to no effect. Just that annoying buzzing noise over and over. This was frustrating, he thought, *We've gotta get out of here, we're trapped for sure.*

Voice announced: *"Fifty seconds to launch."*

"Benicio," Malote stated. "I think we're screwed."

Malote's voice was quivering a bit, and he could hear the anxiety in it. This was unnerving to him as he knew Malote was fearless. He had only ever heard him scared once before, and that had been under another extremely dire circumstance. Looking back over that moment, though, it wasn't nearly as bad as what they now faced. They had never been chased by stormtroopers and soldiers and the cartel at the same time. This place didn't help either. It felt alien. It was a far cry from the local dive bar they enjoyed or even a damn Whataburger at 3am. *How in God's name did this even happen?* He thought to himself.

It was a good question, but not one he had time to ruminate on. He smashed the inoperative door one more time with the butt of his gun. "Why won't this piece of shit open?" He shouted in frustration. The answer came from behind him.

"Because it shuts down when there's less than one minute to launch."

Stunned by the unexpected response, he and Malote both spun around their guns at the ready. The man standing before them was clearly not dangerous. In fact, he looked a little startled as he had suddenly earned the aim of their weapons with his statement. He was dressed in full launch gear, complete with a helmet. The suit appeared to be one singular piece, entirely white, except for a few grey inserts on the shoulders and sides. Other than being white, it looked very similar to the black ones he had seen on the armed men outside. The helmet had a clear visor, which allowed full visibility of the wearer's face. Overall it looked sleek and polished. He could see the man's wide-open eyes through the front of the helmet. Benicio thought the man looked scared, no, startled and alarmed. Yeah, that was it.

"Who are you?" Benicio demanded. "I'm Dave," came the quick, almost friendly reply. "OK, Dave. You're telling me this rocket is about to launch?" Benicio asked.

"Yes. It's going to—"

The astronaut was interrupted by the robotic lady's voice again. *"Forty seconds to launch."*

"Well, you've got to stop the launch right now, Dave." His voice crackled. He didn't mean for that to happen, but the stress was killing him. Doing his best to remain calm. Still, the reality of their situation wasn't only sinking in, it was slamming into him like a wrecking ball. Desperately trying to cling to some semblance of control.

"Sir, I see your gun, but please, you need to listen to me. Do not fire it."

"Stop the launch right now!" Malote shouted.

He stepped closer to the astronaut. Dave carefully raised his hands and took a step back.

"I can't," he insisted. "That can only be done by the Captain in the command deck..." he said while pointing up.

"Then open the elevator... Dave." Benicio shouted. "Do it now!" He was desperate.

"That can't be done either. It's on lockdown, as I just said. You have to—"

"I don't want to hear it, Dave," he replied, Pausing for a second, he had a thought and let out a small chuckle at what he was about to say. *"Fine. Take me to your leader".* Obviously not understanding the ill-timed pun, Dave flashed him a confused look. *"Ugh, your Captain. Take us to your Captain... Stupid!"*

He leveled his gun at the astronaut as he said this. His hands were remarkably steady as the barrel of his weapon kissed the visor at eye level on this astronaut's helmet.

He had no intention of shooting this man. He hated killing, and honesty only drew his gun when necessary or when he wanted to show it off, which was more often than not. He had, however, practiced his menacing pose in front of the mirror many times. Anyone that he would face needed to believe that he would indeed squeeze the trigger. The astronaut in front of him was fully convinced that his life was on the line. The reluctant but highly motivated astronaut motioned to the men to follow him up a ladder at the other end of the compartment. They made their way up a ladder with Dave leading the way. As he climbed into the utility compartment, Benicio looked around. It was a white round room except for an airlock on one side. This was easy to deduce as it was clearly labeled 'Airlock,' and he couldn't help but notice it. The whole space was very modern. It was precisely how he had expected every spaceship he had ever seen in the movies to look. Tavo, still hooded, started climbing, followed by Malote, who was nudging him upward with his gun.

Entering the next deck, he could see that this was the command deck, Benicio, was impressed with its futuristic feel. This was a sleek and smooth room with a series of rectangular wall panels all around. These panels appeared to be storage for computers or who knows what, stored neatly and hidden from view. As the ship was on the ground, everything in the room was sideways. There were a couple of rows of seats facing upward. The first row consisted of four black leather seats that looked like they had been taken from a luxury sports car. They even had five-point harnesses, just like a race car. The second row consisted of two seats, the same as the first, but these were obviously for the pilots. In front of each of them was a single large curved computer monitor.

Each one displayed various telemetry readings. They reminded Benicio of giant overgrown computer tablets. They made for a pretty slick dashboard showing the status of the multiple systems on the ship. He was impressed. He studied the information on them for a second, as he took note of the camera feeds. There were several showing the exterior of the ship from various angles. Between the two front seats, he noted a console with a bunch of buttons and joystick. The whole thing looked more like some kid's gaming battle station or something from a science fiction show. He wasn't sure which. It was not what he had been expecting. He had only seen pictures of the cockpit of the space shuttle on TV, which looked nothing at all like this. The shuttle cockpit was ancient-looking compared to this slick setup. One of the front seats was occupied by another astronaut. This was obviously the Captain. Benicio could tell he had been expecting them as he was angrily glaring back at them, reluctant and annoyed.

"You're not supposed to be here!" the Captain declared as he admonished them. This was no way to treat someone with a gun. He decided he would now aim his weapon at this angry Captain. "Yeah, well, we don't want to be here either." came his retort. "Understood" was the reply, as he said this, the astronaut held a finger up and slowly brought it down onto the console. "Don't shoot. I'm aborting the launch." He was relieved to hear this, but he didn't want these astronauts to know that. He nodded and carefully watched as the astronaut clicked a glowing red button with the word ABORT. As it engaged, it immediately turned green, and the word changed to LAUNCH. On the monitor, an alert popped up with the timer showing 00:10 seconds to launch. It was paused.

Letting out a sigh of relief at this development, he realized that they heard him too. *Oh well*, he thought, *at least we're not taking off*. More relief came over him as he heard distant mechanical sounds of unseen motors powering down. He was starting to get a feeling of being a little more in command of the situation. *OK*, he thought. *This is going to be a regular hostage situation. I can handle this.*

Feeling a little more confident, he motioned to Dave to take his seat next to the Captain. He didn't want anyone to be out of his sight. Since the room was awkwardly vertical, he climbed into one of the seats and motioned for Malote to do the same. Malote immediately grabbed Tavo and clumsily shoved him onto the seat while taking his own. "OK, boss, what are we going to do now?" Malote asked.

It was then that Benicio realized he had stopped thinking ahead. He was no longer planning his next move. The situation had degraded so fast that all he could do and all he was doing was simply re-acting to the events as they unfolded before him. The anxiety started overwhelming him again. He needed to figure this out.

Lightly tapped his own head with the side of his weapon while holding his eyes tightly shut. He asked himself out loud, "Beni, Beni, Beni, What are you doing?", Realizing that he was saying it out loud, he froze suddenly and looked at everyone around him. Realizing that Malote and the two astronauts were staring at him, frozen, waiting to see what he would do next.

"OK, Basta!" he blurted loudly as if he had come up with a plan. He knew he was just winging it, but he wasn't going to let anyone else know that. "We need to get out of here,"

Looking up, he locked eyes with the Captain. "You! What's your name?" he said.

"I'm Mike. Mike Fosum, Captain of the Pegasus. Let me help you." came the reply.

"OK, Mike. Help me. Tell me, what do we need to do to get out of here and—

"Get away from this place?" interrupted Malote glancing quickly at him in an unspoken apology for interrupting his Boss.

"This is not a problem," replied Mike in a calm and confident tone. "There are two ways out of this. We can launch... which I know you don't want, or you can go out the way you came. I promise you we won't get in your way."

"The elevator's broken, stupid!" Malote retorted. Mike, who was obviously feeling the desperation from them, responded.

"No. No. Listen to me. Now that we've aborted the launch, the elevator has been re-activated". As Mike said this, he was motioning to the monitor where the external cameras were. "See," Mike said without looking back at the monitor. "You can leave."

Benicio looked at the screen, and what he saw instantly made him angry. The display was clearly showing the Space Force team getting into the now-reactivated elevator. They were getting ready to come on board.

"Shit!" he exclaimed.

Mike turned around and saw the same thing. "Shit! Shit!" he exclaimed, realizing that this situation was about to get a lot worse.

Malote also looked, and just like his Boss yelled, "Shit, Shit, Shit!" "They're coming to get us!" Malote screamed.

Tavo, under the hood, started laughing, "You guys are idiots. What a bunch of chupa pitos! Hahaha," he mocked. With a quick whack from his gun, Malote shouted, "Shut up! Pendejo!". Malote flashed a glance at his Boss as if to say, "what? He deserved it". He quickly turned to look at Mike again. Mike was sporting a distinct "I fucked up" expression after realizing he had inadvertently thwarted the space force team's stealthy entry to the ship.

"Stop the elevator!" Benicio shouted at Mike. "I can't. The only way to stop the elevator is to initiate the launch." Mike shouted back.

"Fuck!" he shouted. Turning to look at Malote, who was still processing what was happening. He knew they were quickly running out of options. Pausing for a moment, he made up his mind and calmly stated.

"I know a way out." and with that, he shoved the barrel of his gun onto the green LAUNCH button activating it.

Mike shouted, "No! You can't--". "I just did! Strap in, guys! We're going for a ride! Yee-haw!" Benicio didn't know where that sudden yee-haw came from, but *fuck it*, he thought, *this is Texas*.

Now it was Malote's turn to panic. "Fuck... are you serious? Fuck..." he yelled as he scrambled to grab the harnesses.

"It's our only way to get away from those guys. Trust me." Benicio responded, doing his best to sound confident.

"OK, Boss, but hey, how do you buckle this damn thing?" Malote asked.

"...Eight ... Seven..." said the smooth female voice.

"Like an X over your chest along with the buckle between your legs," Mike responded. He suddenly sounded like he was in charge again as he pressed on the various buttons on the screen to ensure that they launched correctly and didn't die right there on the launch pad.

"six...five..." she continued.

Thunderous shaking rose from below as the engines came roaring back to life. The vibrations penetrated every inch of the ship, even the crew. Benicio was frantically slinging the straps over his shoulders and feeling around to adjust the tightness. As he pushed it all together, he heard the click of the belt slipping into place.

"Guys! What about me!" came the shocked voice from under the hood. It was Tavo squirming around and plunging into a major panic attack. He had forgotten about Tavo. *Oh well, fuck him.* "Just hold on tight!" he shouted.

"...Three ...two," the robotic woman's voice spoke up again. *"Have a nice flight... Launch."*

The Pegasus rose with impossible force and speed. He was pushed into the back into his seat. Unable to control himself... He shouted every single curse he had ever heard in his life. No one could hear him as he was drowned out by the thundering freight train-like noise coming from the powerful rockets below. Tavo was shrieking in an unusually high pitched voice, sounding like a little girl screaming, consumed by total panic.

Looking over to Malote, he saw something very different. Something astonishing. A massive grin had spread on Malote's face. He was not panicking at all. In fact, he looked joyous and at peace, and for the first time, he thought, Malote was shining. For a moment, he felt good about his friend's joy.

Of course, that lasted for about half a second before he felt a sudden jolt as the ship rocketed upwards. He started belting out curses at the top of his lungs until he passed out!

A few seconds later, he woke up again. He kept his eyes shut tight, his hands keeping a death grip on the armrests. He struggled to wrap his head around what was happening... Was he actually headed into space? He felt his life flash before his eyes as the Pegasus shuddered and rocked all around him. The sound of the rocket engines drowning out his thoughts.

The engines weren't the only things he could hear. He could also hear Tavo screaming high pitched shrieks that gave way to inarticulate cries, sounding a lot like a wounded animal. He chose to ignore Tavo.

Truth be told, after the initial panic, something unusual, almost magical, was washing over him. He was genuinely thrilled, and commanding forces pushing against him, couldn't dampen that thrill. Even the insane G-forces thrusting him into his seat were feeding this adrenaline rush.

Suddenly, he heard a noise, something like metal being warped or stretched. He had no idea if the things he was hearing were perfectly normal or a sign that the rocket was falling apart or worse exploding. They didn't explode. After a quick jerk, the ride seems to become smoother. Did something fall off the ship? Was that normal? These questions came and went through his head, unanswered. However, he did know that he felt a lot heavier as if someone was pinning him to the seat with a wrecking ball.

Summoning his strength, Benicio forced himself to open his eyes. He looked ahead, beyond the astronauts in front of him. He hadn't seen the portholes when they were on the launchpad. Perhaps they were closed; however, they had opened, and he could see the sky. At first, the view looked pure, a clean blue slate. But it was quickly taking on darker hues, while at the same time seemed brighter and somehow more vivid.

He hadn't realized, but a smile had revealed itself around his mouth. Turning towards Malote, he was hoping to see his long-time companion enjoying the ride. But as he turned his head, the world got swimmy. It was harder to breathe, and he was blacking out. He didn't understand the tremendous G-Forces that were affecting him. His last thought was an image of the ship impacting the ground at full speed, a fiery explosion, and him standing there screaming at it all.

But that didn't happen. No, the Pegasus remained steadfast, thrusting upwards into space. It was Benicio himself that was out of whack. Deprived of oxygen and the forces pulling on him, his mind wandered again as a euphoric feeling took over. He was feeling silly, and although he wasn't aware of what it was called, he was, in fact, experiencing the effects of hypoxia. He welcomed being feeling kinda happy and loopy. It felt as if he was leaving all his worries be-hind. Darkness took over his mind. Closing his eyes as they rocketed, heavenward, he blacked out.

CHAPTER 9

Orbit

Benicio opened his eyes for a moment, he was sure he had arrived in the afterlife. He'd done some deplorable things in his life that made him reasonably sure he wouldn't be welcome in Heaven, but surely that's where he was. Everything was quiet. Serene. Calm. He felt weightless and at peace. There was darkness all around, except for a small bright glow in front of him. Maybe it was the glow of angel's wings or whatever existed after death that had come to escort him to the hereafter.

His mind re-joined his eyes, the effects of the hypoxia had subsided, and he was stirred awake by his consciousness. The glowing in front of him came into focus. It wasn't an Angel. It was just the lights coming from the control console of the Pegasus. Remembering where he was, he quickly glanced once again at the portholes. He could only see the blackness of space, stars in the distance. They seemed brighter from up here. It hit him suddenly, all the events of the last few minutes that had led them to this place. How they had managed to escape the Earth's atmosphere was beyond him, but he realized that they were now in orbit.

Attempting to get out of his seat, he was stopped by the tight straps. As he slapped at the buckle that kept him secured in position, he paused for a second as his weapon drifted slowly past his eyes. Drifting wasn't the right word. It was floating gracefully in front of him, like a ballerina in slow motion. As it did, the gold inlay shimmered as its reflections danced across it. He appreciated the moment, but then immediately reached for the weapon. His hands were trembling a bit, so it took him a second. Securing it back in his belt, he focused on removing the harness. A voice near him spoke, startling him.

"I wouldn't do that if I were you."

He turned to see Mike holding onto a strap attached to the ceiling. He hadn't noticed them before, but there were straps all over this compartment. Mike seemed to be tethered to it, his legs in the air as he floated in the weightless environment. Mike was studying a nearby display in one of the panels that served as the Pegasus's interior walls.

"Why not?" Benicio asked.

"Ever been to space before?"

"Of course not."

"Moving around without gravity isn't as easy as you might think. You're welcome to try, but don't be too surprised if you end up with a headache, or dizzy, or worse, vomiting." He wasn't sure if Mike was a smart ass, or if he was really trying to help him, but he hated being talked down to, and he was pretty sure this astronaut was doing that. He reached for his weapon with every intent to intimidate the astronaut again but stopped when Mike spoke up again.

"Yeah, that's not gonna do you any good up here," Mike responded. "It's safer if you just leave it put away."

"You have no idea who you're dealing with," Benicio retorted. This guy was really irritating him. He was surprised by his own anger. Perhaps it was that he wasn't in control of the situation. He was feeling quite vulnerable and so out of his element, or was it that Mike was indeed in control, and that pissed him off more.

Mike stopped what he was doing on the computer and then turned to face him. When he did, the lack of gravity made it appear as if he was moving underwater only without the water. Mike glanced at the other pilot who was still seated, studying an instrument panel just over his head.

"You good for a minute Dave?"

"All good up here," Dave responded.

Still holding onto the ceiling, Mike looked down at him, much like a disapproving father. It was very uncomfortable, and his immediate reaction was to break out the hostility.

"You! You're not in charge here. I am. Pinche idiota, You don't know who you're dealing—"

"You're right," Mike interrupted "I *don't* know who the fuck you are!" he was visibly upset, "I do know you're not supposed to be here." Pausing to take an angry breath, "How dare you come on this ship with your guns and your hostage. You're some kind of sicario, right? Well, It looks to me like you fucked up big time. You have no idea what you're doing! You have no idea what a huge mess you've made. If you want to make it through this, you will have to cut the machismo bullshit and listen to me. This is my ship, I make the rules! Comprende Amigo?!" Mike was definitely angry.

Benicio wasn't going to let anyone speak to him like this, so of course, his only reaction was to shout back.

"Don't fucking call me amigo! I don't fucking know you! I make my own rules! Sure we messed up getting on your ship, but I have the gun, and that means that I'm in charge. What makes you think you can just yell at me like that. Te fusilo! Pinche pendejo!" He was really fed up with this jackass. Mike was not affected by his speech in the way he had expected; in fact, his defiant reaction really made Benicio rethink his approach.

"You want to know who I am? Well, I'm the guy that's been to space before. This is my domain. I'm the only 'pendejo' who can make sure you make it back to Earth alive. Goddammit!" Mike let out a very frustrated yell. "That stupid gun is not going to do you any good up here. So...yes, you'll listen to me and obey my rules if you want to live. And one more thing," he paused for a second "Call me, Captain!"

Benicio was shocked at this bold display of aggression. But he also respected it. He knew the astronaut was right. He really did have no idea what was going on or what he was going to do. Thinking about what this stranger had just told him, he knew what he had to do next... and what he did next surprised the astronaut.

He broke out in laughter, flashing an almost too friendly smile at this stranger. "All right, vato." he started, "You know what? Not many stand up to me like you just did. That tells me you're no punk. I can respect that. So here's what I'm going to do. I'll listen to your rules. No guns. But only if you promise to get us back on the ground," he paused for dramatic effect, "and I mean right now!" Standing his ground, he added, "And one more thing... I ain't calling you Capitan" Both men stared at each for a second. The battle of wills was at a draw.

Malote started coughing, which broke the tension. Looking over to check on his friend who had blacked out. Benicio was about to say something to his friend, when out of nowhere, Tavo floated into view, blocking his view of Malote. He was still passed out, his bound hands floating in front of him, he had started to float up as he wasn't buckled in. "Son of a ..." Benicio cursed, as he pushed Tavo back into his seat. He then did his best to secure the hostage in place. As he did so, he looked back at Mike and said. "How fast can we get back? I've got to deliver this guy to my boss pretty soon."

"No can do, compadre," Mike responded. "You boys don't know what you got yourselves into. This ship is on its way to the International Space Station. There's supposed to be some elite soldiers here to take care of some trouble at the ISS. But you guys went and totally fucked that up pretty good. Besides, the Pegasus isn't like a car. We can't just cut a U-turn and head back to Texas. We have to wait for our next re-entry window. And that's only problem numero uno."

"What's numero dos?" Benicio asked.

"This launch was very last minute, as such, we didn't load it with enough oxygen for a full trip up and down on the next re-entry window. We need to get additional oxygen if we are going to make it back. If it was just Dave and me, we'd be fine, but we aren't quite sure we're going to have enough oxygen for all of us. We only have enough to get to the ISS to—"

"The what?" He interrupted.

"The ISS. The International Space Station." Mike nodded, "Once we get there, we can dock and get all the oxygen we'll need."

"Ok. I understand that but.." He raised a single eyebrow as he inquired, "Who did we mess up? Why were they going to the ISS." Benicio replied, trying not to sound too ignorant about all this space stuff.

"Like I said, I have no real idea. All I was told was that we needed to relaunch the moment the space force arrived. Everything was perfectly timed, right down to the second. From what I gather, you catapulted your fucking truck right into the middle of a critical military operation and sent it all to hell."

He grinned for second as he recalled that last jump before hitting the fence, "Heh, heh, heh, That WAS some sweet air I got... but... this is not my fault, and you can't—"

"Stop. This is absolutely one hundred percent your fault. You not only stole this spacecraft and launched it, but also sabotaged a top-secret military operation that was critical to national security. When we *do* get back to Earth, and IF you survive this, you're in some deep shit."

Benicio hadn't had time to process the gravity of the situation. He knew he'd have El Gallo's men waiting for them... and if this astronaut was telling the truth, the United States government might have a bone to pick with him too. *Well, Shit,* he thought to himself. *We've really done it this time.* Of course, that situation seemed kind of far away, and he needed to focus on immediate problems.

"How long until we get to the ISS?" Benicio asked.

"It's a matter of how many orbits it'll take to reach her altitude. Our launch window was good, but not optimal, we are traveling in the same direction as the station. We're likely looking at just under four hours."

A voice from Benicio's right surprised him. Glancing over, he saw that Malote had now come to. He was obviously captivated by watching Mike float around. He looked like he was watching some sort of magic trick. "I knew that," Malote stated, still groggy from the black-out. "But there was a rocket in Russia that launched not too long ago....made it in like two hours, right?"

The smile that flashed across Mike's face surprised Benicio. "That's right," he said, obviously impressed with Malote's odd nugget of information. "That was the Soyuz capsule. Back in 2013. You know about space flight?"

Malote shook his head. "Not really, but I do watch the news sometimes." He continued, "You know, I always wanted to be an astronaut when I was a boy. Lance Armstrong was sort of my hero."

"You mean Neil?" Mike corrected him.

Malote's sense of wonder instantly disappeared, replaced with a sudden outburst of anger as he replied: "You know what the fuck I mean."

"Tell me then, since you know a lot about space," Mike said in an admonishing tone, "Would you have been smart enough to *not* bring a gun on a rocket?"

Malote looked to Benicio with an *oh-shit* sort of look. Looking back at Mike sternly, almost indignantly, he said, "I'm not stupid. These guns are our tools, and we don't go anywhere without them." He continued, "It's like this rocket. I saw the 'roadrunner.' This is just like the ACME rocket the Coyote strapped himself to. Shit is dangerous, but it's the tool the Coyote used for his work." Would you go to work without your tools? I didn't think so. So fuck you. Don't mess with my tools." Malote retorted with a rather unusual perspective.

Mike responded. "First of all, we have much better rockets than Wylie Coyote. Second, I care because one bullet through the hull will decompress the vessel, killing everybody, including you." Mike retorted, "So you tell me. Does that sound like fun to you?"

"Well, how about—" Malote started.

But he stopped himself. His face went slack for a moment, his eyes growing wide as something caught his attention through the porthole.

"What is it?" Benicio inquired. "Malote, what's wrong?"

Malote shook his head as if trying to believe his eyes, slowly nodded as if asking Benicio to look in front of them. He did so and saw what Malote was looking at. Instantly understanding why his friend was transfixed.

The Earth had crept into view. He watched as his friend craned his neck to see more. Malote was awestruck. Benicio smiled as he realized that the unexpected majesty of the planet had tugged at his friend's emotions. It was a rare and wonderful thing to witness. There was no other word for it. At that moment, Malote forgot about the mess they were in. He existed only in the present, no past, no future, just the beautiful moment. He watched as Malote's eyes got wet, but didn't let a tear escape.

Malote gazed at the planet, its pure shape, it's distinct colors, and he felt immeasurably tiny. "Look at it," Malote stated, his voice small and innocent. "It's beautiful."

"It is," he replied to his friend.

"Imagine...me seeing the same things Lance Armstrong saw."

"Neil," Benicio corrected.

"Fuck you."

Those words hung in the air as the cabin in the Pegasus fell silent. They were caught in the wonder of the serene and peaceful beauty of the planet beneath them.

CHAPTER 10

General Mayhem

The Pegasus launched for the second time in under ten hours, taking with her three incredibly unprepared passengers. The Space Logistics headquarters was in utter chaos. Garrett Parker had watched it all unfold.

The Pegasus' powerful rockets had ignited, sending the helicopters and the wrecked truck, tumbling clear across the launchpad, like paper in the wind. The team that was supposed to be on the Pegasus had been stuck inside the disabled lift. He couldn't believe it.

How could a couple of locals have messed up the mission so catastrophically?

Of course, no one had foreseen that there would be a security breach at the facility at that precise moment. The commander in charge of the space force team was on his way up. He didn't have any right answers for the man. Still, first, he had pressing matters to attend to,

namely, establish contact with the Pegasus and find out who the hell the three stowaways who had hijacked his Pegasus were.

"Do we have communications with the Pegasus," he asked the flight director.

"We're in contact now; All systems are green. Telemetry indicates launch occurred within our window. We only have health stats on our two astronauts. Unknown to the others. Captain Fosum requested that we wait another eight minutes for mission briefing." the man responded.

"Good. Well, at least that's some positive news." Garrett responded, adding, "Escort the Space Force Commander to the war room. We need a new plan." Glancing at the mission clock, he continued. "We need answers. Ask Captain Fosum to figure out who our guests are."

"Yes, Sir, right away." the flight director responded before exiting the office.

Knowing he needed to somehow salvage this mission, he felt an incredible amount of stress. *This is going to be the longest eight minutes of my life*, he thought.

***

Approximately sixty miles above the Earth, Benicio was enjoying the ride. He wasn't sure if he was still feeling the hypoxia, or if it was something else. Still, he had a good feeling about their situation. He glanced over to Malote, who was utterly enthralled with the view out of the portholes. Tavo caught his attention as he was starting to move around. As his prisoner regained consciousness, he immediately started hyperventilating.

"Hey, calm down vato," Benicio told Tavo as he tried to calm him with useless words. Almost immediately, he watched as Mike made his way over to the hyperventilating man to assist him. Benicio had been studying Mike's movements in the weightless environment. He figured floating around couldn't be that bad. In fact, he was really looking forward to it. The moment Mike's attention was focused on Tavo, he unlatched the buckle at his chest. Almost immediately, he felt himself floating up out of his seat. It was a surreal feeling, like being tugged gently upwards by someone that had your stomach tied to a tether.

It was a little scarier than he thought it would be. He was moving his legs, but it had no effect. The sensation was weird. Making a swimming motion didn't work either. *This is wild*, he thought. Finally, he pushed himself off, using one of the seats for leverage. He instantly floated across the small room to one of the walls. He knew that anything resembling a smile on his face looked odd and out of place, but he allowed one to briefly cross his features. It did not escape him that he was experiencing something that very few people got to feel. Now he understood why the walls were lined with the padded compartments. They were there to keep people from hurting themselves in this environment. He chuckled for a moment as he recalled that he thought these cushions were only for crazy people in insane asylums. "Hmm, Makes sense," he mused.

Mike, still preoccupied with Tavo, turned to him.

"What?"

"I guess you have to be a little crazy to go to space," smiling as he said it.

Malote started chuckling.

"You look like a fool," Malote stated.

"Feel like one, too." came the reply.

Malote unlatched his buckle too.

"You too? You don't know what you're doing." Mike said, feeling a lot more like a babysitter than he wanted to.

"Yeah, I don't know what I'm doing out here in space, but I figure, if you can do it, so can I."

"Are you guys really this stubborn?" Mike asked, clearly irritated.

"Sometimes."

"My God ...just...just don't touch anything. If you need help getting around, use the handles along the walls."

Benicio used them as he was still not used to the weightlessness. He pushed himself towards Mike and Tavo, a strange sensation started in his stomach. For a moment, he thought he was going to get sick, but he managed to shove the feeling away. He floated over to Mike, doing what he could to keep his stupid grin off his face.

"How is he?" Benicio asked.

"He's fine, blacked out again. He's going to have an awful headache when he wakes up."

Benicio nodded, taking a look around the Pegasus. Realizing that he knew absolutely nothing about how it worked. *Yeah*, he thought to himself, *I need to befriend these astronauts. It's the only way to get back to Earth.*

"Dave, how much time do we have before the briefing?" Mike asked.

"About three minutes."

"Ok, Thanks," Mike responded.

Turning his attention to address everyone there, Mike motioned for everyone's attention.

"Listen up." He began, "You two geniuses and your hostage have placed us in a difficult situation."

Benicio was about to protest, but the look in Mike's eye's told him to wait.

"In a minute, we're having a briefing with the command control room... with our bosses." Mike took a moment to make sure everyone understood the importance of his statement.

"For the moment, We are proceeding as planned. We will rendezvous with the ISS for Oxygen replenishment. However, I want everyone here to know that it is incredibly important that whatever command control wants us to do, we are ready to comply. That includes you two." Mike said, pointing at him and Malote.

Benicio responded, "Look, man, as long as you're gonna get us back on the ground, we'll help. What do you need? Do you want us to carry the tanks in? No problem."

Mike looked a little flustered, "Tanks? What? No, that's not how this... You know what." He suddenly smiled as if to placate him. "Yeah, Ok, Thank you."

Benicio nodded back, although he felt that Mike's response seemed less sincere and more sarcastic.

"It's critically important that when we are briefed that you don't argue with command." Mike was pointing at the main displays behind him. "This is a life and death situation. We need to follow whatever instructions they send. Am I understood." Mike stated in all seriousness.

"Yeah, man, whatever," Benicio responded. He knew his contempt levels were registering in his response.

Looking back to Mike, he added: "Your one of those people who needs a plan for everything, huh. Yeah, I know your type. Sure, we'll work with you, after all, I wouldn't want you to lose your shit" Benicio sounded pretty confident in his assessment. Mike was taken aback by the sudden and accurate insight from Benicio.

"However," he continued, "We need a few things, too."

"Really, Like what?" Mike asked incredulously.

"When we get back home, Malote and I are to go free. No cops, no spooks."

"Hey, I don't have any control over that. God only knows what sort of a mess is going on down below. All the agencies are probably already down there, just waiting for you assholes to come back."

"Shit." Malote interjected, "He's right, boss." as he darted a concerned glance at him. At that moment, the Communications channel sprung to life, a voice could be heard calling the ship.

"Pegasus, come in. Boca Chica Calling. Over."

Mike immediately motioned everyone to take their seats as he settled into the captain's chair. The men complied.

"Boca Chica, this is the Pegasus, we read you loud and clear," he responded.

"Pegasus, we are switching to Alpha Victor Charlie. Over."

"Boca Chica, Switching to Alpha, Victor, Charlie. Acknowledged." Dave was pushing some buttons on the console. Benicio couldn't help himself, he had to ask. "What's Alpha, Victor, Charlie?"

Dave answered without looking. "Alpha Victor Charlie is our encrypted video feed. It stands for Audio Video Channel. It's what we use when we don't want anybody listening in."

Dave didn't see it, but he had nodded in acknowledgment. Benicio wasn't sure how this was going to play out. Knowing that whoever was going to be on that call was going to see their faces. Unsure about how he felt about this kind of exposure. He worked better in the shadows, anonymously, like a ghost. Not liking this development, but he realized that he didn't have much choice.

The video display came to life. To his surprise, he saw a large conference room table. There appeared to be engineers and uniformed military men on both sides of the room. At the head, was that guy, what was his name? Right, Parker. Garratt Parker, the owner of this whole thing. Just then, some unseen voice could be heard saying. "We're on. Go ahead,".

A second later, a General came onto the screen. He was a lot closer than all the others. He must have been standing between the table and the camera. His intense glare looked right through them. It was unnerving.

"Gentlemen, I'm General Eastman. I need a sitrep from your end. Speak." He commanded. This man came off as a no-nonsense kind of guy. His face was stone and unreadable as he finished talking. This is really weird, Benicio thought to himself.

Mike spoke up first, "General. I'm Mike Fosum, Captain of the Pegasus. Here's our sitrep. We had made final preparations for our mission to escort Space Force personnel to the ISS. All systems were a go. However, we were intercepted by the three gentlemen you see behind me. They are armed. They took control of the Pegasus and initiated the launch before the Space Force team could board. No one has been harmed, and they are..." Mike paused for a second to glance back at the trio before continuing. "Compliant." Benicio let out a quiet scoff as Malote whispered back, "Compliant my ass." Mike instantly gave him an angry glance. Malote didn't realize he said it loud enough for everyone to hear. Immediately he looked down and away as if he hadn't said anything.

Ignoring this exchange, the General cleared his throat. "I see," he replied. "Well, I don't have time to fuck around. As we are still in the middle of a critical mission, even though those... " he paused for a second, "Gentlemen... have set us back. We must complete our task." As he finished the sentence, someone offscreen handed the general a sheet of paper, obviously some kind of update. He glanced at it, glared back at whoever gave it to him. "Really?" he admonished them, although, at what, Benicio had no idea. The general looked back at the astronauts as he cleared his throat once again.

"Ok. Here we go." He started. "What I'm about to tell you is Top Secret. I've been authorized to read you in. A few hours ago, terrorists in India stole and launched a rocket, the ISRO Chandra. They released a video in which they announced their intention to seize control of the ISS and weaponize the.." he paused as if he couldn't believe what he was about to say. "Snow Cone." Benicio and Malote couldn't help it. They burst out laughing. "Snow Cone! hahaha!"

The General instantly shut them down. "This is no laughing matter!" Benicio and Malote, immediately calmed down, forcing their smiles away. The General continued. "The Snowcone, or as everyone else calls it, the 'Snowcone of Death' creates 'dark matter.'

It's safe in space, but if it ever reaches Earth, it can potentially decimate entire continents. These terrorists have announced that this is their intent. They are going to use it to destroy the United States." The General looked at everybody again. He wanted to make sure they understood the seriousness of the situation. Nobody on the Pegasus was smiling. In fact, Malote's jaw dropped as he absorbed the magnitude of what he just heard.

"As you can imagine, we must not let this happen." Benicio's face had become stoic. He realized how bad they had fucked up, but he was seeing an opportunity at the same time.

"The Chandra and her crew are on a similar orbital pattern to the ISS. They will reach it at approximately the same time as the Pegasus. We need..." The General paused again, this time, he looked up to the ceiling as if he was once still not believing what he was about to say.

"We need you. All of you, to stop the terrorists at all costs."

There was silence on the Pegasus.

Mike and Dave gave each other shocked and somewhat fearful glances. The same thing happened with Benicio and Malote. Feeling the need to break the tension, Benicio was the first to speak.

"Excuse me, Mr. General," he said. "But are you fucking crazy? You want us to go kill some terrorists? This isn't our fight. No. No, no-no. You can have your ship back. We'll take it back, you can have your guys come back up here and do that. Leave us out of it."

Benicio sounded more scared than angry. However, as he said this, he glanced away from the screen to Malote, winking as if to let his friend know he was up to something.

"Son, you have to do this. You're already there. There's no time for you to come back. I hate this too, but we don't have a choice here." The General responded.

Those were the words he was waiting to hear. Benicio sat back in his chair as if he was pondering the General's words. Finally, he spoke.

"All right, Mr. General. Let's say we do this for you. Let's say we solve your problem. What do we get out of this?" He smiled a bit as he said it. He knew he had the leverage to negotiate. This was probably going to be his only way to escape the situation and be free again. Malote, glanced at him, smiling as he finally understood the play.

The General looked furious. He was obviously not expecting this to be a negotiation.

"Listen! you!" He paused as he looked down at some of his documents. "You are Benicio Elodio Del Angel. AKA 'El Fenix' You are a felon, a fugitive and you are sicario. You've been affiliated with several cartels. As far as we can tell, you are currently working for the Texas Houston Cartel. Your buddy there is Apolonia Mendoza AKA 'Malote'. Also a sicario. Both of you have served time for smuggling, are wanted in connection with at least a half dozen kidnappings, and you are persons of interest in a few executions. We know exactly who you are. You're going to do this because your alternative is prison. Yes, you are going to jail for the rest of your lives! Who the hell do you think you're fooling with." He glared at them as he finished. Benicio thought the man was going to pop a blood vessel in his eye.

"Hahaha," came an unexpected laugh from Malote. Turning to his friend, he asked, "What?"

"Your name! Hahaha, your name is Elodio. C'mon man, I didn't know that was your name. haha." Malote laughed harder. "Elodio del Angel! Ha!"

He didn't like being made fun of, but he knew which buttons to push, so he responded. "Ok, APOLONIA!" to which Malote instantly stopped laughing and retorted.

"Hey, not funny, they named me after my grandma."

"I know, right? Now shut up, I'm negotiating here."

Looking back at the General who was not amused at their reaction, Benicio responded.

"I get it, you know who we are." He smiled as he said it. "But the way I see it," He slowly pulled out his impressive hand cannon.

"We have what you need. We're your only option." He kissed the side of the barrel. Looking back at the disbelieving General before him, he continued.

"We're not only Sicarios. We're independent contractors. Businessmen. Let's make a deal."

Benicio was feeling comfortable, as this had become familiar territory. He was used to negotiating with cartel bosses, and they were usually ruthless psychopaths who would kill him for absolutely no reason. This General might be angry, but he was much less crazy than those people.

"We'll go to the ISS, and we'll kill the bad guys," He stated nonchalantly. "A contract like this should only run you two..." Malote tugged at him while gesturing the 'up' signal... "No, Four. Yes, four million dollars." Malote blurted, "Each!" He nodded in agreement, "Yes." he continued. "We want four million apiece, tax-free. And we want our records cleaned. No jail." Malote whispered in his ear. Benicio looked back at him and responded,

"Really?" Malote nodded.

Looking back at the General and said. "We also want a new truck. Something made in Texas. Yeah, with all the bells and whistles."

The General was angry, no, he was furious. He seriously looked like his eyes were gonna pop out of his head. Slowly his demeanor relaxed. Perhaps he had accepted that he didn't have much leverage over them as he thought. But he did calm down after a few moments. He finally responded, although he was speaking through clenched teeth, he managed to say.

"Agreed."

"I'm sorry, I didn't quite get that. What did you say?" He was beaming. He knew he had played them, and although this was still a tough situation, at least now there was a light at the end of the tun-nel.

"We agree to your terms." The defeated General repeated.

Benicio smiled.

CHAPTER 11

The ISS

Approximately two hundred and fifty miles above Earth, at the International Space Station, Commander William Yelland had just finished his briefing with the officials at NASA. His stern face failed to hide his deep concern over what he'd just learned. Activating the shipwide intercom, he took a deep breath, doing his best to sound serious, but not alarming.

"All hands, report to the MLM immediately."

Looking through the recessed storage bins, he located the Station Evacuation Protocols Manual. As he studied it, one of the crew members, Geo, floated into the MLM.

"What's up boss," the astronaut inquired quite casually. Not looking away from the manual, Yelland answered, "Not until everyone is here." Geo had expected the response. "You were in the Copula again, weren't you?" Yelland inquired. He already knew the answer.

But before Geo could respond, Roy came floating in and greeting everyone with "Sup."

Yelland glanced up disapprovingly at Roy,

"Why do you have to always be so casual? My CO back in the Air Force would have reprimanded you for responding like that."

Roy flashed him a smirk, "Well, I guess it's a good thing we're not in the Air Force."

Geo responded, "Smartass." to which Roy pretended to take a bow while replying, "Thank you, I'll be here all week." In the weightless environment, his bow turned into a full rotation head over heels before he steadied himself on one of the walls.

Yelland looked up from his reading, and looked around, asked, "Where's Karen?" He already knew the answer. She was a feisty scientist. And like most scientists he knew, she was probably lost somewhere inside her head.

"Roy, go get her. This is important."

"What's important?" The question came from the smooth female voice as the attractive scientist floated into the module.

Not missing a chance to be a smartass, Roy responded to Yelland, "She's right here, boss." Yelland just glared at him.

"I just got off the comms with NASA, and you're not going to believe this." He paused for a second to ensure that he had their complete attention.

"About three and a half hours ago, The ISRO reported an unauthorized launch of their latest rocket, the Chandra. It seems that terrorists have taken her and are headed to the ISS to take control of the snowcone and eject it to Earth."

All jaws dropped in disbelief. Quickly, lifting a finger to keep them silent, Yelland continued.

"The Pegasus was launched from Space Logistics down in Brownsville, Texas, to rescue us, but..." He paused again. Nobody was breathing.

"It seems that it was also hijacked by Sicarios who are also headed here."

"Ha!" mocked Roy suddenly, "Good one boss. You almost had me until you said Sicarios. It's not the best joke, but I'll give you points for originality."

"Dammit, Roy! I'm not joking," Yelland shouted.

"Wait, you're serious? All that really happened?" Roy wasn't joking around anymore.

"We've been ordered to lock down the ISS, do what we can to impede the terrorist, and de-man the station via the Pegasus. The Sicarios have made some kind of deal where they've agreed to help us." As he said this, he realized that he hadn't processed this part yet. Confusion spread over his face for a second. Before realizing that his crew had also not fully absorbed the information. They just kind of floated there, in shock.

Clapping his hands hard to snap them out of it, he yelled, more like a drill sergeant than a station commander.

"Come on, people, let's move! We have approximately twenty minutes before they get here!" He maintained a stern look but what he was really experiencing was panic. Something his crew could not know..

"Roy. I need you to EVA. You have to disengage the external locks on the docking mechanisms except for this one." He commanded as he pointed to the nearest node. Roy nodded and quickly headed to the nearest airlock.

Turning to Karen, Yelland ordered. "I need you to turn off the snowcone safely without causing another flashing. If you can't, we have to launch it into space. Whatever happens, we must not allow the terrorists to get their hands on it."

Karen was about to protest, but the look in Yellands eyes told her that this wasn't the time. Instead, She nodded, as she sped off towards the FSL which housed the snowcone experiment.

"Geo. You're with me. We need to secure the experiments and shut down all the research projects. We start at the far end of the station and work our way back here, we're closing all the modules, and making sure all the orbital rooms are isolated." Geo, while still shocked, acknowledged.

Yelland couldn't recall the last time he'd worked so quickly and so quietly in his life. He turned for a second to watch Geo, who was typing away at a furious pace at a nearby workstation. They were systematically shutting down and locking every single module. He hadn't done the math but knowing the ISS was about the size of a football field and contained sixteen different modules. Most of them carried experiments. At this rate, they had about one minute per module to get it done. No way they'd be able to get them all, but they had to try.

Checking in on Roy, Yelland activated his earpiece. "Roy, come in, How's it going out there?" he asked as he continued to multitask.

"I've checked the three available docks, but I can't seem to disable them. Not without knocking out some of the other systems." Roy responded.

Yelland was a little frustrated at this news. The station was designed to allow ships to dock with it. It was never intended to deny anyone entry. Of course, nobody could have foreseen the current state of things.

"All right, Roy. Acknowledged. Get back inside and help us shut down the compartments."

"Right away, Boss."

A few minutes later, they were joined by Roy, who must have broken a speed record in getting out of his EVA suit.

"All right guys," Yelland said, "I'm going to go check on Karen and the snowcone. Work fast, I'll see you at the MLM."

"Yes sir," came the response, almost in unison. Yep, Yelland was proud of his crew. Sure they joked around a lot, but when it came down to work, they were all business.

He quickly left the module and floated through the crowded passageways to the Kibo module. As he arrived, she was there, true to form. He could see that she was transfixed on her creation. He knew this discovery was important, not just for her but also because of the great mysteries they were solving. Her breakthrough was as big a leap forward for humanity as Tesla's alternating current or even the moon landing. As he pondered this, he floated next to her at the snowcone's controls.

"Well?" he asked, "What are the options for this thing?" She had been transfixed, keeping her head still as she looked through the observation scope.

She turned to face him with tears in her eyes. She was obviously distressed and worried.

"Oh come on now," he tried to comfort her. "Don't do that. There's no crying in science." His attempt at humor fell flat. She was taking short breaths, exhaling longer in an exercise to steady herself. All he could do was be there for her. At least for the next two minutes anyway.

Finally, she took one long breath, looked him in the eyes, and spoke.

"We have three options," she said in a monotone voice. "Option one: We eject the dark matter into space, causing another flashing event." Option two: We don't eject it. If the field around it destabilizes, it may still flash, but the snowcone's explosion will destroy the station."

"And what's option three?" Yelland asked.

"Option three: Is to push this button right here," She pointed to a small panel attached below the main apparatus which contained a small digital display and a single orange button. "It's something I've been working on." Then she quickly added, "It's never been done, so I don't know if it will work." she continued. "Pushing this orange button will activate a 'force field' around the dark matter powered by the molecule itself."

"Um, Ok, Force field?" Yelland asked, not understanding what she was talking about. Now she seemed slightly annoyed that she had to explain the concept using smaller words. Yelland imagined that this is probably why Einstein resorted to humor. It was easier for him to deflect theoretical physics inquiries by telling a joke rather than just using terminology in his head. on so-called noobs.

Karen, clearly flustered a bit, continued.

"Think of an egg. Got it?"

"Yes"

"Ok, now, the dark matter is the yolk of the egg. The eggshell is the force-field, and it's powered by the albumen. Got it?"

"Yeah... sure.... Um, what's the albumen?"

"Oh jeez." She was clearly frustrated. "The clear part of the egg!"

"Oh, I got it. So let's do that. What's the problem?"

"The problem," she explained, "Is that this eggshell might exist in two dimensions simultaneously. If I activate it and exist in the other dimension only, then we'll be ok. But if it occurs in both dimensions, it might rip a hole in time-space, or worse, it could still destroy the station."

"Wow, that sounds really bad? Why would that even be an option?" Yelland was beyond confused.

"The good news is that it will prevent another 'flashing' from occurring. Technically it would still happen, but the 'eggshell' would limit the flashing to the inside of it only. Also, I don't know how big the eggshell will be. It might take out this lab when it occurs. Understand?"

"No, but I'll take your word for it," Yelland responded as he tried to wrap his head around what she was explaining. "All right, so you're saying is that our best option which happens to maybe be our worst option is to push the orange button and cross our fingers?"

She smiled. "Yes, now you've got it."

He wasn't quite sure he did have it, but he really didn't have the time to argue. Besides, his head was starting to hurt from all this thinking.

"So, what do you want us to do?"

She was looking around, lost again in her thoughts when she suddenly locked eyes with him again. "You said Sicarios were coming to rescue us. We need to make sure they succeed, and we have to keep the terrorists away from the snowcone. But if it comes down to the wire and can't stop them, one of us needs to push this button."

Yelland sort of understood. The orange button was a hail mary. If everything else failed, they would push it.

"Yelland, come in." His comms lit up as Roy interrupted his train of thought.

"This is Yelland. Go ahead, Roy."

"They're here. We can see the ship coming in on final approach, you better get over here right now."

"Which ship is coming in?" He asked.

After a small pause, he got an answer.

"Um... Both of them?" came the reply.

CHAPTER 12

Arrival

Amari watched in awe, eyes transfixed on the beautiful approaching space station. Her solar panels glistened in the reflected sunlight. Feeling more confident than ever that his mission was going to succeed. He knew he was at the threshold of greatness. He'd avenge his lost love and successfully terrorize the western world, and his name would go down in history.

Managing to look away from the beautiful sight, he turned his attention to the cramped passenger compartment. Evaluating his crew, noting their expressions were a mix of excitement and fear. *No matter,* he thought, *They'll be well motivated once they board the station.* He had confidence in his men and he felt proud of them. Strapped in, his seat, which was directly behind the pilot, was slightly uncomfortable. It was not much more than a small metal frame covered with thin cushions. As he adjusted himself, trying to get comfortable, he thought, *I guess the ISRO wasn't too big on luxury. Doesn't matter, this will suffice.* Checking his sidearm, a Glock 19, he recalled how this weapon had been gifted to him by a Syrian commander after a successful raid. The weight and feel of the gun made it his favorite. He gave it an affectionate squeeze as he smirked quietly to himself.

"Macchar," Amari addressed to his right-hand man and pilot. "How long until we arrive." Although Macchar was a man of few words, he was sharp as hell and often underestimated. The man was staring straight ahead, focused on his task, and ensured they remained on target. Without looking away, he responded, "Seven minutes." Amari smiled as he thought, *Brief but precise. The man is a gem.* Leaning forward to try and see the station better, he addressed the hacker sitting next to Macchar.

"How are we doing, Jarah..." This man was more of a geek than the rest of men; however, he was unequaled at accessing computer systems and was basically a genius on all things communications-related. Amari trusted him, but for data, more than 'wet work.'

"Can we establish communication with them?" Amari asked.

"We should be able to, yes," came the response. Amari, smiled as he turned to address the three fully armed men behind him. "My loyal friends and fellow crusaders. We are approaching the enemy. Soon, we will meet them eye-to-eye. This is necessary to gain control of this space station, I am determined to live or die with all of you to achieve this. As long as we fight united, no one can beat us. They can send their special forces, but we know their tactics. They can't beat us. At the end of this day, We'll celebrate our victory on the ISS! And if not, We'll celebrate in heaven for we are the Zalam Jihad! Allahu Akbar!" Shouted Amari.

"Allahu Akbar! Allahu Akbar! Allahu Akbar!" Cheered his crew! They were pumped and clearly excited. Ready for whatever was waiting for them.

"Amari, sir, excuse me," came the somewhat timid voice among the cheers. It was Jarah. Motioning Amari to come to check his screen.

"What is it?" he inquired.

"Military tactics, sir. I've analyzed the layout, and based on our approach vector, I think the astronauts have a chance to escape. The other ship will be arriving at the same time. If those are special forces on board, then there's a good chance they'll exit onto the outside of the station to sabotage our ship or ambush us". Jarah sounded concerned, as he continued.

"Sir, I think it's a trap."

"I see," responded Amari in a much more pensive tone. Looking back at the fired up crew, he commanded. "The battle is upon us. You three suit up! We have an ambush to bust! They have underestimated our tactics once again. It's time to show these Americans what it feels like to have a real jihad rain hellfire on them!"

"Yes, sir, right away!" shouted the men as they put on their EVA suits. These were, of course, standard-issue ISRO spacesuits. Gray and utilitarian, not much to look at, but they worked great for what Amari needed. Leaning forward to speak with both Jarah and Macchar. "When you're close enough to the station, get us close enough to disembark the men onto the struts without being noticed."

Jarah, eyes brightened up. "Ah, I see., We can do it but will have to use manual control. We'll activate the automated docking computer after they unload. It will make our approach a little more complicated, but I'm sure we can do it." Jarah said as he glanced at Macchar. Macchar glanced back, nodded, and proceeded to do something with the flight computer.

Turning to look at his men, he addressed them. "Gentlemen, The Zalam Jihad is going to do some extraordinary things today. You are going to be our first wave. You'll surprise the enemy, intercept them before they can lay a trap for us. Keep them busy outside while we infiltrate the station. It's risky, but trust in your equipment, your tethers, and your brothers, and we'll meet back up inside the station, victorious!"

Ansari watched as Macchar successfully completed the orbital maneuvers and watched as they closed in on the giant solar panels. The word close wasn't enough to describe exactly how close they were. He could see the tip of the Chandra's winglet was now maybe 5 feet from the exposed truss segment at the end of the array.

Amari, having already motivated his men, ordered them to exit onto the winglet located just outside the small cargo bay behind the crew compartment. Ensuring that each soldier was equipped with a rifle and a tether with a carabiner attached, he instructed them. "Once that light turns green," he said as he pointed at the indicator above the door, "depressurization will be complete, Open the latch, and you'll be able to access the ISS. Tether yourself to the trusses, make your way up the station, and eliminate anybody out there. We don't want surprises when we dock."

He continued. "Am I understood?" "Yes, Sir," came the response. Knowing that his hand-picked soldiers were the best men he had back on the ground. Amari was confident that they would succeed up here. His worry was that not only were they battling the Americans. They were fighting in an unfamiliar hostile environment, Space. He was determined to succeed, Shouting one last encouraging mantra for his men.

"Remember! Allahu Ackbar!" he shouted as he shut the door to the cargo hold and initiated the depressurization sequence.

As he did this, the men shouted back, "Allahu Ackbar!" He placed his hand on his chest. Their devotion was heartfelt. He watched through the porthole, as a sudden, somewhat cheerful chime, indicating that the depressurization was complete. "Go time," he said, although the comms were off, and they could hear him. He watched as the door shifted outward for a split second before unseen motors slid it to one side on hidden rails. Turning on the comms, he expected to hear more cheers; instead, the only sounds he could hear was the fast heavy breathing of these once tough men.

No one had exited the ship. Suddenly, a voice came over the comms uttering a single word. "GO!" Macchar had announced decisively.

Immediately, Ansari watched the men funnel out the open hatch and onto the Chandra's winglet. They were stepping cautiously on the smooth surface.

Once the last soldier was outside, Macchar immediately activated the door control, shutting it instantly. There was no turning back for these men. A growingly frustrated Ansari watched as the soldiers looked around. He shook his head in frustration as he realized that they hadn't seen the ISS. They had expected it to be lying right on the winglet. They were now warily looking down over the edge. "It's not here! There's no station!" screamed one of the men. As he did so, he stepped back towards the hull. No sooner had the words left his mouth, when all of a sudden... Clank! The back of his helmet had struck something above him.

Amari threw his hand up in defeat as he watched this ineptness unfold in front of his eyes. Over the comms, everyone heard the clank and turned to see what it was. There stood the astronaut trying to collect himself, with his hand up holding on to something to keep his balance. That something was Truss from the ISS. It was no more than a few inches above from where they stood. This was the first time anyone had looked up.

He watched as they discovered the ISS in all her glory. She resembled some kind of majestic holy relic floating silently above them. They just stood there in awe of the thing that was larger than they had expected. The stunned men just stood there gazing at it, wrapped in wonder. "Guys? Guys!" Jarah interrupted their moment. "We're on a tight schedule. Get up there! Now. Hurry"

Snapping out of it, one of the men responded. "Right away. We are heading up." One small hop later, and the first soldier was climbing up the truss. Followed quickly by the other two.

A moment later, the Chandra thrust forward, continuing on her way to the docking station. Relieved that his men had successfully mounted the station, Amari declared.

"I believe it's time we announce our presence."

CHAPTER 14

Arrival Part 2

Benicio couldn't remember ever being so happy as he performed a weightless backflip inside the crew deck of the Pegasus. He knew it probably wouldn't be easy, but he had made the deal of a lifetime with the military and was in the midst of his celebration. Malote had joined him, and the two men were playing like two ten-year-olds in a bouncy house as they bounced off the walls.

Benicio couldn't help noticing that Dave and Mike kept glancing back at them. He wasn't sure if it was to make sure he didn't break anything, or because they wanted to join them and have fun in the weightless atmosphere. Of course, they couldn't because they were busy navigating to the ISS. Never completely letting his guard down, he carefully watched the astronauts as they completed a maneuver to course correct the Pegasus.

Malote was definitely overjoyed. He had let out a "whee!" *which he suddenly cut off* as he tried to compose himself. He was definitely enjoying this way too much. Not only was he living out his childhood dream, but they had just made the deal of a lifetime. They had a new mission that was going to pay off bigtime.

Although Benicio was a hardened criminal, he wasn't completely heartless, and he had a strong belief in karma. He thought to himself that he probably would have helped these astronauts for free, but he was happy to have had the foresight to make a deal. As he took a second to take in the situation, he knew that this was the calm before the storm. He and Malote would have to step up and have the battle of their life. His face grew serious as he floated over to Dave and asked, "Do we know anything else about these bad dudes we've got to take out?"

"Still no idea," Dave said. "And that's the truth. You know what we know. We should assume the worst. We know they hijacked the Chandra, in India. They'll be arriving at about the same time as us. We also know there's six of them, and they're armed. I think they are probably after the Snowcone of death."

"You mean, the Snowcone is real? Ha! I knew it!" Interrupted Malote before Benicio could motion to him to shut up.

"Ok, so what should we expect," Benicio asked in all seriousness.

Dave glanced over to Benicio; "I'd expect a fight."

"I can handle a fight,"

Malote's interrupted again with a laugh, he asked: "Yeah, but in space?" he mocked.

"He's right," Mike said as he agreed with Malote. "I've seen you moving around in here. It's not very graceful."

"What about guns? Can they fire guns in space?"

"Yes, guns can fire in space."

"It would be small arms, most likely," Dave added. "No RPGs or anything like that. Something useful in close-quarter combat. Automatic weapons would be crazy dangerous. They would just destroy the modules, and that's just suicide."

Benicio took in what these astronauts just told him. Sighing deeply, he replied. "Ok, So we go in, we 'take care' of these guys without missing, save the Snowcone and the astronauts and go home. No problem, we got this."

Mike and Dave shared an uncertain and surprised glance. "It could work. Still, we need to make a plan." Benicio rolled his eyes. These astronauts still needed to try and do things in a much more specific way.

Dave started, "Once we initiate the docking procedure, we will need to immediately begin transferring oxygen. As we are doing this, Mike, you go ahead and assist Yelland and the crew in getting onboard. Benicio and Malote will head to the far side and do what they do." He glanced at Benicio as he said this. "If they make it back, we'll perform an emergency detach procedure and head back to Texas." As he said the last part, Benicio could see the astronaut had relaxed a little bit. He chuckled a little as he thought about how often he and Malote had gone into a situation with a plan, and how it never worked out. In his experience, he knew they were better off winging it. At least that way, his enemies couldn't anticipate his next move. *But if that's what this wero needs to feel better, then ok, we'll let him think his 'plan will work,* Benicio thought to himself.

Malote had apparently lost interest in the conversation. Benicio expected this as his buddy was usually down for whatever came next. After all, that was their Modus Operandi. He noticed that Malote was just looking straight ahead, past the pilots and through the porthole. "Is that it?" he asked.

Benicio looked in the direction of Malote's gaze and saw a flickering white light in the distance. It was brighter than a star and seemed, somehow, more real. When his eyes locked on it, Benicio could tell that it was much closer than any of the stars in his field of vision.

"Yeah, that's it," Mike replied. "That's the International Space Station." They sat in awed silence, watching the ISS come closer.

"Hey, what the hell is that!" Malote blurted out, breaking the silence.

Mike and Dave quickly got on their consoles and were checking the sensors.

"It looks like the Chandra. Shit, they've arrived before us." Dave said suddenly. Mike responded, "I'll make contact with the ISS, see what's going on over there."

CHAPTER 13

Time to go to work

Two minutes earlier, Yelland had been taking a lesson on how to stop the Snowcone from falling into the wrong hands. Now he was rushing to the MLM with Karen right behind him to handle the next crisis. *No time to panic, just keep your people safe. Keep the Snowcone away from the terrorists and get on the Pegasus*, he thought to himself. This was stress. Upon arriving at the MLM's Comms unit, Yelland was thrilled to see at least one familiar face on the screen. He and Mike Fosum had spent quite a bit of time together training at the Kennedy Space Center.

"Man, oh, man, am I glad you see you, Mike!"

"Likewise. Although I wish it was under better circumstances," replied Mike.

"Well, you're aware of the situation, right?" Yelland said.

"Yes. Houston read us in. Terrorists have hijacked the ISRO's Chandra and are coming to commandeer the ISS and the Snowcone. Sounds about, right?"

"Sounds dead on," Roy stated over Yelland's shoulder.

"As long as you didn't bring any terrorists, I'm glad to see you."

"Well," Mike said. "Funny you should say that. We don't have terrorists. But we did kinda get hijacked by two cartel guys and their prisoner."

Roy, Karen, and Geo all laughed nervously at this obviously ridiculous notion. Yelland, however, did not. He knew Mike well enough to know that the look on his face was all business. Somehow, as ridiculous as it sounded, Mike wasn't kidding. Feeling the anxiety welling up in him, he responded.

"Seriously? What happened?"

"Well, long story short. We were waiting for the Space Force Team, but through a strange series of events, we launched with three Sicarios instead."

"Wait," Karen said. "Is he actually *serious?*"

"Afraid so," Dave said from next to Mike. "The good news is that they seem to be fairly benign and have cut a deal with the military to help us out." Crack! At that moment, the video screen showed the barrel of a gun knocking Dave's helmet. "I'll show you benign right here, Puto!" Shouted Malote. "Ow!" Dave retorted. "I didn't mean benign like harmless; I meant it like.. like.. you're a badass on our side." "Hrrrg, OK," grunted Malote as he moved back out of view.

Yelland, clearly surprised by the sudden outburst, responded, "Absolutely not. You think I want terrorists and some common street thugs on here with—"

"Wait a fucking minute!"

Yelland watched as a hardened-looking Mexican man appeared in front of the screen. He nearly pushed Mike out of his seat as he made sure he was in the center of the screen. "You don't know me! There ain't nothing common about us. You know what vato. Fuck You! We're here to save your ass—"

"There's no need for that," Yelland interrupted. He was doing everything he could to remain calm. To say this was an unprecedented situation was laughable. NASA has teams of engineers whose job is to think of all scenarios and come up with contingency plans to avoid surprises. But this was a scenario that not even the most paranoid engineer would never even think of coming up with. They had no protocols for a situation like this. It was all on Yelland's shoulders, he was going to have to wing it, and he was going to have to pretend like he wasn't freaking right the hell out.

"You all may know how the rockets work and about sciences and things like that," Benicio retorted. "But violence is my language. You say you've got some bad vatos coming on board. I'm the guy you're gonna want in your corner, puto! Remember that when you want to act all superior and talk down to us."

Yelland swallowed every retort that sprang to his tongue. Pushing aside the fear that was very quickly starting to bloom inside of his stomach, he replied.

"I read that loud and clear. This is a stressful situation for everyone, and, quite frankly, we may actually need your help. We don't have time for insults. The Chandra is docking on the far side of the station as we speak. How long before you can dock."

"Two minutes?" Mike stated.

"Acknowledged. There's something else, Yelland. Where do you want us?" inquired Mike as he was busily doing something with the computers. "Our plan is to have you maneuver and dock directly with the MLM.

"Roger that" We can do that. We'll meet you at the MLM; however, this causes a new problem for us. Mike."

"What?" Yelland couldn't believe this. What else could go wrong today? "Talk to me, what's the other problem."

"We left Texas without enough oxygen on board for us to get back. We are currently at about 12%. We're gonna need to refill the oxygen tanks. The PMAs have built-in oxygen refueling lines, but that's not the case on the MLM. We're going to need to run a line." stated Mike.

"Crap," Yelland responded. "We're gonna need more time then." He already knew they were cutting it close, but oxygen is pretty necessary.

"Can you slow them down?" Inquired Mike.

"No, not really," Yelland responded as he motioned over to Roy.

"Suit up. You're going to have to EVA to tether the emergency oxygen transfer hose from the ISS to the Pegasus." Yelland commanded. "Yes, sir!" responded an enthusiastic Roy. Yelland was surprised by the enthusiasm, but he knew Roy loved going outside, it was terrifying and exciting, he lived for it.

"So that leaves one other question," Karen stated.

"What's that?" Mike asked.

"Are we abandoning the station? Leaving it in control of terrorists? Or are we going to do anything to get rid of them."

"Both, I think," Dave replied. "Our top priority at the moment is getting you out of the station. We definitely don't want them to have any hostages. The second priority is to keep them away from the Snowcone. If we can't, then we have to disable everything. "

"Got it. There's just so much important science happening up here." Karen lamented, "I'd hate to lose it and the station."

"Hopefully, it won't come to that," Mike said. "but we need to get everybody out of there before the terrorists take hostages."

"Everybody clear?" Yelland asked.

Karen nodded, and Roy responded, "clear." He also heard a murmur of agreement from the Pegasus through the video screen.

"Uh Guys, not so fast," came an unexpected response from Geo. Looking around, Yelland hadn't realized that Geo had left the MLM and was in the Copula. Whatever he was seeing, Yelland knew it wasn't good. "What is it, Geo?"

"Well, it looks like we have three bad guys making their way up the aft truss through the solar panels. Looks like they're headed towards us."

"Damn," Yelland uttered, thinking that the situation couldn't get any worse was the wrong thing to think. Because apparently, it could.

"Pegasus, did you hear that?" Yelland was hoping for a hail mary at this point.

"Yes, we heard. Three hostiles coming up the aft truss." Mike replied, sounding grave.

Yelland looked up at the comms screen, just in time to see the sicario in the back, nodding to his buddy. Benicio turned to the screen and yelled back, unnecessarily loud, "Orale vato, We got this! Malote's volunteered to go out there and take em out." Malote's eyes grew twice their size, but Benicio gave him a look that shut him up before he could protest. Mike and Dave looked a little confused but obviously didn't have a better idea. Dave looked at Yelland and shrugged his shoulders as he nodded.

Yelland sighed for a second, then realizing they were out of time, he responded with renewed conviction.

"OK, Do what you do." Then turning his attention to Mike, he continued,

"Let's do it, then. I'll be sending Roy outside to prep for the O2 transfer. Roy to get the airlock."

"Roger that. Godspeed, everyone."

With that, Mike terminated the video call, leaving Mike with his crew. Roy was already suiting up in the airlock. He looked happy, which was good. Yelland supposed everyone was feeling the same way *he* was feeling. Yes, he was scared shitless, but the adrenaline pumping through his body was damn near intoxicating. He felt a lot more confident now that they had put together a plan, and it looked like this was really going to work.

"Roy, Make sure you transfer as much O2 as you can as quickly as you can. Pegasus is our life raft away from this mess. And I'd hate to successfully evacuate the ISS only to suffocate halfway home."

"Roger that, Boss. I'll top it off." Roy responded. He had already suited up and was working the airlock on his way outside.

Yelland was watching him on the monitors and checking his watch. If everyone's calculations were correct, they had no more time as the Chandra would be docking now.

CHAPTER 14

Suit Up, Vato

Benicio looked around the Pegasus as she was preparing to dock with the ISS. Still not accustomed to weightlessness, he felt slightly dizzy and very uneasy. Focusing on the activity at the center console seemed to settle the dizziness. As he watched, Dave was working the controls, and for a moment, it reminded him of a video game. He watched as Dave kept one hand on the tiny joystick on the black center console, and with his other hand, was tapping on the display to activate who knows what system. A box on the screen zoomed to fit the entire display, it was a video stream from a camera mounted on the front of the ship, perhaps on the docking port. Featuring a sizable red crosshair, he watched as the computer overlayed a yellow crosshair on the ISS docking mechanism. Dave was very carefully moving the joystick to align the two crosshairs. As he did, Benicio could feel small vibrations from the maneuvering rockets adjusting the ship's approach. It looked easy enough. Perhaps he should have played more with his gaming console.

"Are you serious?"

His best friend Malote interrupted his attention.

"You want me to go out there?"

Turning his attention to his friend, he snapped back to the situation at hand. Just a moment ago, they spoke to the Commander of the ISS. Commander Yelland had informed them the bad guys were docking. He told them that they had spotted three bad guys on the outside of the station. They were making their way towards the Pegasus. He had a knee jerk reaction to the news and had just volunteered his friend to go outside and take out the incoming bad guys.

"Yeah, This is what we do. We get hired to kill bad guys. Those are bad vatos. What's the problem?"

"Boss, but outside? Like in outer space? I don't know if—" Malote sounded worried.

"Do you trust me?" He replied, knowing the answer.

"Do I trust you, Boss? C'mon man, you're the only one I trust. Well, you and my old lady." Saying this as he clutched his lucky medallion."

"You said you always wanted to be an astronaut, right?"

"Yes. But this is not how I thought it would be."

"Here's what we got to do," Benicio said in a more serious tone as he placed his hand on Malote's shoulder.

"These guys don't know bad guys like we do. Some bad guys are coming our way. We can't let them stop the astronaut outside from getting us the air we need to get home. I want you... No. I need you out there with this vato to make sure he does what he needs to do. If shit starts, I need you to take care of it. Think of this as your chance to be a hero." Squeezing his friend's shoulder as he said the words, adding, "Besides, you've got your girlfriend here to protect you" He grabbed the medallion out of Malote's hand and held it up, "See. She's beautiful, and she'll make sure nothing happens to you." Malote seemed semi convinced. Benicio's words were comforting to him, but was it enough to overcome his fear?

Mike had been listening in on their conversation and turned in his seat to face them. He reached out and tapped Benicio's arm to get his attention. The man had a scowl on his face, but Benicio thought he saw Mike wink at him for a split second, but he wasn't sure.

Suddenly, Mike started shouting, "That's absolutely ridiculous. You want him to fucking go outside?!. You're Mad! Absolutely nuts! We train for months just to learn how to maneuver out there. You don't have any training. You're not even astronauts for god sake!"

Benicio glared back at Mike, as they made eye contact, he instantly caught on to what the man was doing. It had apparently worked because Malote's fear and insecurity was giving way to his anger and desire to show these stupid astronauts that he had what it takes. Malote glared at Mike with a newfound resolve.

"I'm doing this. There's nothing you can do to stop me." He retorted, speaking through his gritted teeth.

"You heard him" Benicio responded to Mike, "Look, we get it, it's hard, but trust me, Malote can do this. Train him. Tell him what to do. I've seen the movies, it can't be that hard." retorted Benicio

"Yeah." responded Malote, "I mean, Hell, yes!" Obviously responding to a sudden adrenaline rush. "I wanna do this!"

"Hey, boss?" Malote said after a moment of reflection. He appeared like someone who would have had weak knees were it not for the weightlessness hiding it. "I don't know, man. Maybe he's right. Or maybe it should be you. You've got nerves of steel."

"Malote, you're never gonna get a chance like this again. You do this, and you'll be a REAL astronaut. A real astronaut hero!" Benicio reassured his friend.

Sudden laughter interrupted them. For a moment, Benicio thought it was Mike or Dave laughing. However, no, the mocking laughter was coming from Tavo, still buckled into his seat, hands were still bound. Benicio had nearly forgotten about the little pissant.

"Him? An astronaut? You guys are crazy! A hero? Hahaha, Estan *locos! You guys are idiots."* He mocked.

His laughter was like needles to Benicio's brain. And, truth be told, he had a lot of frustration building up inside of him. At that moment, Tavo had given him the excuse to let that frustration out! He pushed himself back to Tavo's seat. Drew back his fist and slammed it hard into Tavo's chest. The lack of gravity made the punch very awkward. Instantly propelling Benicio back and into the back of the pilot's seats. He was a little stunned by the unexpected motion, but still, it had the desired effect. Tavo cried out in shock, or was it a mixture of laughter and pain. It didn't matter. Benicio's frustration was relieved, and that idiot was in misery.

Looking back at Malote, he said. "You ready to get this done?" A nervous smile crept across Malote's face. "Yeah, I am. I'm no chickenshit!" Malote motioned his fist towards Tavo as if to punch him, but stopping short. Tavo instantly flinched. "I ain't no idiot either, pendejo."

"You heard him," Benicio said, looking at the pilots. "Now, help him suit up?"

Mike unbuckled himself and motioned the men to follow him as he made is way down the back of the compartment towards the payload area. As they entered the circular room, the lights instantly came on, revealing this very sparse compartment. Almost the entire circumference of the room was covered in white padded cushions cleverly hiding compartments with small recessed latches. As Mike activated one of the neatly recessed controls, the panel in front of him rotated out of sight, revealing a glass door. This was the airlock. It was a small tubular room with a door on the opposite end, which led outside. None of it really seemed like that big of a deal until Mike opened up an adjoining panel revealing a sleek futuristic looking spacesuit. It was not as bulky as they had expected. This suit was white except that it sported streamlined orange inserts on the shoulders and around the neck. It looked more like what a racecar driver would wear rather than an astronaut.

"OK, boys, now listen up. This isn't your standard spacesuit. This is our experimental EVA suit. We're testing it as a possible prototype for our planned moonbase." Mike stated proudly, forgetting for a moment that they weren't astronauts. For a moment, Malote looked like he was going to be sick as the reality of the situation hit him. Just then, Dave made an announcement from upfront.

"Roy's outside ready to run the line. I'd hurry up if I were you."

"Let's just focus on the suit," he said, taking the suit and turning to Malote,

"Listen closely. I'm about to give you a crash course on this suit and spacewalking. We don't really have time, but I'll make it quick."

Mike did his best to assist Malote in getting the suit on. Malote removed the pistol he had in his belt and handed it to Malote. This spacesuit was turning out to be a tight fit. Mike was going over the various features of the spacesuit. "Here is the pressurization status readout. As long as it's green, you're good... and this one, this is the communications and biometrics readout. If this starts beeping..." all this information that started to make Benicio uneasy. He certainly hoped Malote was listening, but, at the same time, he did not want his friend focusing on all of the scary shit Mike was saying.

"When you get out there, you're going to feel very disoriented. Just focus on looking at the ISS. Don't look out into space, or even earth. Doing this will keep you oriented. Out there, you're really going to feel the lack of gravity, more so than in here. It'll screw with your inner ear, and your balance is going to be all messed up. You may feel the need to puke. Don't. Trust me, you *do not* want to puke in your spacesuit. The tether attaches here." Mike continued while tugging at the umbilical attachment bracket. This is your lifeline. You must try not to move too fast. You move the wrong way or get into any harsh physical contact, the tether can get knotted or, in extreme cases, frayed. This would be bad. There will be handholds, like metal ladder rungs, that run along the length of the ISS; I highly recommend you use them. Is all of this sinking in?"

"Hell yeah!"

Apparently, the instructions and warnings had done nothing more than wipe away Malote's nerves. He now looked incredibly excited, much like a kid about to hop on a roller coaster. "You see this, Benicio? I'm about to be an astronaut like Lance Armstrong!" Malote announced through the massive smile on his face.

"Neil," Mike corrected.

"What? Hell no, I don't kneel to anyone but my lady!"

"Not *kneel!*" Mike said. He was trying to sound stern but also trying to hide a laugh. "Neal! It's Neal Arms— You know what, never mind."

"Whatever man," Scoffed Malote. He shook the whole exchange off as Benicio caught a child-like glee in his eyes.

Moments later, Malote was wholly suited up. Weirdly, Benicio felt pretty proud of him. Forgetting for a moment all the crappy events that led them to this impossible situation and now, there was Malote, about to live out his boyhood dream.

Mike inquired to Dave, "How long?"

"Anytime now. We've achieved a soft seal, Yelland is initiating the pressurization and completing the hard seal from his end."

"Got it. Keep me informed," Dave replied as he led Malote to the airlock.

"Woah, wait!" Malote yelled. "We can't do this! Not yet!"

"Why? What is it?"

"My Skinny Lady! Shit! Benicio, I don't have her. Where is she? I can't do this without her!"

Benicio had nearly forgotten that he had taken the precious charm earlier in the main cabin. He glanced upwards toward the command cabin and spotted the medallion floating in the air, slowly catching some light, almost signaling him with the shiny reflections.

He quickly drifted over to it and carefully embraced the precious Santissima Muerte medallion. Taking it back to his friend as if it were a precious holy relic.

Unable to get it inside the spacesuit, he instead managed to loosen the chain and slip it around the helmet, securing the chain under some velcro straps. "Here you go, my friend. She's right here", he said.

"Oh, man." Malote gasped as he lifted the medallion to his face and pretended to kiss it.

"We almost messed the whole thing up just now!"

"You think *that's* what might have messed it up?" Mike asked sarcastically.

"One more thing," Benicio said as he took out his precious Desert Eagle. "Take this, it's much more powerful than your gun."

"Are you insane?" Interrupted Mike.

"He's more likely to hurt himself. I mean, what if he shoots it at the station! Do you even know what that would—" "Shut the fuck up. This is important!" Benicio cut in as he pushed Mike back. Benicio then turned to Malote, and as he stuck the piece into one of the utility pockets near his waist, he said in a much lower voice. "Don't shoot the ship or the station, OK?" Malote responded with a nod. "OK, Boss"

"For God's sake, if you do have to use that, be careful with it. We don't want—"

"I remember," Malote interrupted Mike just to shut him up.

"Malote, you good to go?" Benicio asked.

Benicio responded with a thumbs up and a huge smile. There were nerves in that smile, but it was clear that he was excited.

"Closing the airlock," Mike said.

Malote was now locked in this tiny room, waiting for the depressurization process to finish so he could open the outer latch. A small part of Benicio wished he was the one going. But then, as the latch opened, the expanse of space was revealed, quickly squashing those wishes. Space was overwhelming. The lack of atmosphere made the stars brighter. Suddenly, the realization of how small and insignificant one is made this a visceral shock.

"Over the comms, they could hear Malote's breathing. It had become quick and heavy as he stared at the open latch he was about to exit through.

"Malote, Calm, your breathing. Take a deep breath while counting to five. Hold it. Then exhale while counting to five again. This will help you calm down." Mike said, "You're going to feel the weightlessness right away. Just go with it. And for God's sake, whatever you do, do not touch the umbilical unless you absolutely have to."

They could hear Malote's breathing stabilizing as he followed the instructions from Mike. After a few seconds, Malote responded, "Hey, that breathing thing really works. I got this", Malote said with a confident grin.

"OK," Dave announced. "Here we go. Hard seal in three...two...*one.*"

CHAPTER 15

Spacewalking

Roy loved going outside the ISS. One of his favorite "go-to" answers to solve any of the routine issues was "No problem. I'll go outside and fix it" He had performed numerous oxygen transfers and minor structural repairs. Once, he had to replace one of the glass panels on the Cupola after a meteorite strike. That was pretty exciting work. The spacewalk part of this transfer should be a piece of cake—well, except for the terrorists.

Today was a little different, he thought to himself, as he worked his way over to the Pegasus, Roy felt a little uneasy. He was very aware that he was in plain view of the bad guys, and for a second, he imagined a literal target on the back of his spacesuit. If that wasn't awkward enough, the Pegasus was sitting beautifully in front of him. The liferaft to get out of this situation wouldn't go anywhere if he didn't complete this critical undertaking. But this life raft had cartel thugs on board. The image of the angry cartel guy holding the gun on the viewscreen earlier was burned in his head. "Wow, he thought, this is so insane, it's almost funny."

Roy had attached the O2 line to his suit. He made his way up the trusses on ISS towards the Pegasus. He heard a crackling in his helmet from the comms system. At the same time, something caught his attention, right along the edge of the Pegasus, which made no sense at all. However, before he could react, he heard Yelland's voice.

"Roy, This is Yelland, Over."

"Roy here. Over."

"I know you don't need another challenge, but—"

Before Yelland could finish, Roy's eyes locked on some movement on the outside of the Pegasus. He now saw what it was, but still, something about this wasn't quite right. His mind was racing to make sense of it.

He watched as someone floated upwards out of the Pegasus, decked out in a spacesuit, reverently rising away from the ship. Arms at his sides as he was gazing up. It was not unlike an angel floating up towards the heavens. It was majestic. He could see a golden medallion around his neck, catching the light and glistening in its glory. Wait. Was that a gun sticking out of the front of the suit? Roy was taken aback. He squeezed his eyes shut a couple of times in disbelief of the astonishing sight before him. Suddenly the spell was broken. The majesty of the scene destroyed as the figure's arms started wildly flailing, scrambling to grab the umbilical. The man was attempting to maneuver themselves back to the ship's surface, scrambling to grip one of the trusses on the ISS. Whoever it was definitely didn't know what they were doing. It was almost comical.

"Who the hell is that?" Roy asked.

"That's one of our new Mexican friends. They've got this crazy idea that they can help with their guns."

"That makes no sense."

"I didn't think so, either. But according to Dave, this one is sort of agreeable. He figures it might be a nice insurance policy to have him out there with you if things get dicey."

"Is that a gun?" He replied aghast, already knowing the answer.

"I'm afraid so."

"This is...this is... nuts!" It was all Roy could think to say as he continued working his way towards the Pegasus while watching the flailing figure, now inverted and doing what he could only describe as a lousy attempt at breaststroke in a futile effort to get back down to the ship.

"I know," Yelland replied as if he was reading Roy's thoughts. "But stay focused and do a good job. We're all depending on you, Roy."

As Roy drew closer to the gangster, he held his hand out, trying to motion for him to stop. He even yelled it out but realized that they were not on the same comms channel. "Hey, Yelland, can you get Dave to tell this moron to stop moving and just stay put? He looks like a baby duck learning to walk out here. He's gonna make this whole transfer that much more dangerous."

"Roger that."

Yelland apparently worked fast. A few seconds later, the would-be astronaut stopped his gyrations and was just floating there quietly, slowly spinning to face Roy. As they made eye contact, Roy could see the man looked somewhat relieved. Roy gave him a little wave.

Roy tugged the transfer line along behind him. He was tethered to it, so it was more than just the means to save the crew on the Pegasus; it was literally his lifeline. He had to be careful with it because it was very much like a fireman's hose. It could get knotted up and caught on just about anything on the side of the station.

Roy had reached the Pegasus and was face to face with the awkward stranger. He had stopped flailing and was just floating quietly while holding the tether in one hand.

"You, Roy?" the guy asked.

"Yes."

"I'm Malote."

"Okay. You...are you okay?"

"Yea, I'm fine."

Malote and Roy stared at each other for a moment as if to measure each other up. Roy was a little taken aback to see the fascinating combination of joy and ...was it fear? Or anger on Malote's face. Roy gave a quick glance at the weapon Malote was carrying. Just for a second. He hoped Maloted didn't notice. But he had. Instantly his expression turned to mean as he grabbed for the handle. "Hey, No funny business, okay pendejo? This isn't for you, so don't even look at it."

Roy raised his hands to appear unthreatening. "Don't worry about me. I get it. It's just a lot bigger than I thought." Malote let out a hearty laugh. In his head, he was thinking. "Yeah, That's what she said." He thought for a second about actually making the joke but then thought better of it. Yeah, That would definitely not be appropriate.

Roy observed the range of expressions coming from Malote and chuckled as he also thought the same response might have been triggered. Both men had seemed to have bonded at that moment, finding common ground in an unspoken corny joke.

Roy pulled on the O2 umbilical. He was opening the panel on the Pegasus, which hid the mechanism for the transfer. Because of his experience at doing such tasks, Roy looked at home as he deftly maneuvered around the craft, much like a seasoned mechanic working on his favorite car. Malote did his best to keep up with him but moved much more like a fish out of water.

"Hold up, wait for me," Malote said as he struggled to stabilize himself along the rungs.

"You're aware that we don't have time to hold up," Roy replied. "You know there are bad guys headed over here, right?"

"I do, smart ass. I'm just getting used to this shit, alright.." Malote retorted.

Roy latched the hose onto the mechanism and turned it until the clamps clicked. Pressing the transfer switch, the tube started to inflate, not unlike a water hose. Within a few seconds, the digital readout lit up next to the valve. The numbers on the readout started to rise, starting at nine, ten, then twelve. The oxygen transfer was progressing quickly, and with any luck, it might not take as long as they had been fearing.

"C'mon, Really, That's it? That's all you had to do?" Malote mocked. "Shit, I could have done that," Roy ignored him. They both knew there was a lot more to it than just that.

"Roy?" It was Dave from the Pegasus. There was a lot more worry coming from his tone than Roy had expected.

"Dave, I'm here. The O2 transfer has been initiated. You should see the progress on your end."

"Yes, I see the transfer. Good job. but..." The transmission trailed off.

"Yeah. But what?" Inquired Roy, "What is it now?"

"Not to alarm you, but you need to hurry up. The hostiles have reached the modules and are making their way over to you, and it looks like.... yeah, it looks like they're armed."

You've got to be kidding me, Roy thought.

"Oh, sure. Why the hell would I be alarmed about that?"

Sure enough, as he looked past the ISS airlock he had used to come outside, just beyond it, he saw the shapes of two men scrambling off the trusses and scaling the modules on their way towards them. Like his own 'would be' partner, these guys also had guns, or were they rifles?

It didn't really matter. All Roy knew was that this situation had just gotten a lot worse. There were now three armed men out here with him. The number of things that could go wrong had only escalated. This was not a pretty picture.

"What the hell do we do now?" Roy asked, a little less calm and more panicky than he wanted to let on.

"Right now, You need to focus on the O2 transfer. We'll keep an eye on them and come up with something.... but.. just in case, and I can't believe I'm saying this..." Yelland responded." Given the trouble headed your way, I think you should let your new partner handle this. Good luck out there."

Roy was in total disbelief. *They were screwed. What a clusterfuck this was.* Glancing back to the oxygen readout, which had reached forty-four percent. Yelland had told him to top it off but, at a minimum, get it to at least eighty. No way was going to happen before the terrorists reached them. He needed to do something. He knew what needed to happen. Roy reached up with a free hand and grabbed Malote's shoulder.

Malote, who had been focused on the gauges in a vain attempt to keep from panicking, looked up and made eye contact. Without saying a word, Roy rolled back and looked towards the incoming intruders. Malote followed Roys glance and instantly saw the men.

Alarmed, Malote immediately altered his stance. He moved past Roy and made his way to the trusses to get a better grip on the ISS. To Roy's surprise, Malote instantly transformed from a clumsy first time spacewalking civilian and was now prowling like a hunter sneaking up on his prey. The man now had a singular focus. His free hand had instinctively reached for the Desert Eagle.

The intruders were facing the Pegasus, steadily moving towards them as they closed the distance.

Roy estimated there might be fifty meters between them.

The oxygen gauge clicked up a bit more, reaching fifty.

This is going to get ugly, Roy thought.

CHAPTER 16

Battle

Malote's attention had shifted to focus on his targets. All thoughts and worries about his spacesuit and the dangers of being in a vacuum left his mind. This was war, and he was now in his comfort zone. He had acquired his targets and knew what he needed to do. The rest of the world, the ISS, Pegasus, even Roy, were out of his head. He was hunting.

Positioning himself as best he could along the trusses, he tried to conceal his position. Although he knew that his tether was giving him away, there was nothing he could do about that. His primary focus was on watching these men coming towards them in their gray spacesuits and weapons. From what he could see, they weren't tethered like he was. They had long lanyards attached to tether points on their suits with a large carabiner, which they used to clamp on the trusses. Watching as they slowly made their way up the station towards the Pegasus, noting that they also seemed to be carrying much more substantial weapons. Not sure of the caliber, but he surmised that they were probably fully automatic rifles. He focused on the two of the men that were headed straight towards them.

However, he noted that the other seemed to be trying to flank them from the right as he could see the astronaut heading for the far side truss. He needed to keep an eye out for that guy. *No surprises,* Malote thought.

Wrapping one hand tightly around the truss, he carefully aimed at the closest soldier. The only sound he could hear was his own breathing, He slowly exhaled, squeezed the trigger and fired. His gun let out a quick flash, and he instantly felt the kick from the weapon. Just for a second, he was confused at the lack of sound. His eyes caught the ejected casing tumbling quietly and quickly away. He'd forgotten that this was the vacuum of space. The next second, his confusion was replaced with sheer panic as the effects from the recoil thrust him backward and away from the ISS. "FUUCK!" Malote shouted as he found out firsthand why everyone was making a big deal about weapons in space. In a single horrifying second, he was suddenly and unexpectedly launched off the station flying past the Pegasus, past Roy, and into the empty space beyond it all.

Less of a reaction and more of a primal panic provoked him to let out a litany of cuss words that would have made most sailors blush. "Puta! Pinche Madre! Pendejo! Hijo de patada! aaaahhh, ahh, ahh!" He wasn't even sure he was making sense, either. He hated that he did it, but Malote went from badass hunter to screaming like a schoolgirl. He was tumbling out of control into space, spinning crazily in all directions. For a moment, he saw his entire life flashing before his eyes. His Santa Muerte medallion slamming onto the faceplate, almost mocking him, reminding him of the death to come.

But death didn't come. His out of control tumbling came to a sudden stop as the tether reached its end, becoming tight. For one sickening moment, Malote was sure it would snap, and he would go floating out into space. Realizing he was still screaming, and as he regained his composure, the sound coming out of his mouth just faded into silence.

"Malote! Breathe! You have to chill. The tether is still attached, you'll be fine. but you have to calm down!"

He was pretty sure it was Roy's voice. Still, the unfamiliar voice did very little to ease him. He didn't know this, but he was only about 25 feet away from the station, but it felt like he had tumbled for miles. Malote practiced the breathing exercise Mike had recently taught him. As his breathing returned under control, he was able to look around and take in the view. Floating at the end of the tether, away from everything, he was able to see the Pegasus, Roy, The ISS, the bad guys, and the Chandra all in one take. Perhaps for the first time, he noticed the big beautiful blue sphere that was the earth below them. His brain overloaded, and he started to panic again.

"Please! Help me! auxilio! auxilio! Ayúdenme pendejos!"

"I know it's scary as hell, but you need to chill the fuck out *right now*. You hear me? Calm down. You're hyperventilating."

"Okay. Sorry. Yeah, I hear you..."

"I can pull you back, no problem, but we gotta hurry. Those assholes are still headed this way." Those assholes are still headed this way. "You need to take care of these guys before they kill me, I mean us!"

Malote already felt the tug on the tether as he was being pulled back down by Roy. He didn't like this awkward sensation as he felt pretty helpless.

"You good now?" Roy asked as he was drawn in closer and closer back to the ISS.

"Aye, I'm good. Did I get one?"

"No, not quite," Roy responded with a small laugh. "But, hey. You didn't hit the space station. And what a ride, huh? Man, you flew off this sucker faster than a.. .hahaha.. faster than a speeding bullet. Good Job, superman."

Although Malote hated to be made fun of, Roy's words were just what he needed to calm down. And, of course, he would never admit it, he had found it funny. He felt much better now. Thank God for the tether. He would have been a dead man for sure.

Roy had nearly pulled him all the way back when Malote noticed that one of the terrorists that had been branching off to flank them, had dropped to one knee. He was busy securing himself with a much shorter tether. It told Malote everything he needed to know: they knew what they were doing...and they were about to open fire.

"Faster, faster!" Malote yelled.

Roy pulled harder. As Malote was almost back, he had focused on the other bad guy he had shot at. He was also securing himself to the truss and preparing to fire. "Shit," Malote uttered. "They're gonna shoot at us. Fuck!"

"Listen to me," Roy responded. "If you can shoot these assholes, I think I have an idea so that you don't fly off the station again. What do you say, superman?"

"For sure! What is it" Malote didn't want a repeat of his previous folly.

"Okay. Have you ever seen skydivers in a tandem?" Roy uttered.

"What? The fuck are you saying.." The imagery was lost on Malote.

"Okay, nevermind," Replied Roy. "I need to tether you *to me. I'll* hold on to the station, and will keep you from flying away." See these clip-looking things on the sides of your suit? We'll tether ourselves together, and you'll be able to fire."

"Oh, I get it," Replied Malote, although he really didn't.

"I'm going to give you one more tug. When I do, I'm going to spin you around and clip my suit to your suit. Ready?"

"Yeah, I think—" responded Malote, but before he could finish, Roy had given him the last tug and in one deft movement, had spun him around and in front of him. Now both men were facing the same direction, and Roy had clipped the carabiners shut. They were now tightly harnessed together. "Hey! What the .. Nah man, this isn't cool. We look like a couple of P—" Malote had started to protest. "Look!" shouted Roy. "They're gonna start shooting any second now."

Malote tried to pull away as he really didn't like this sudden extreme close proximity to Roy. Way too intimate for him. Swallowing his pride, he accepted it, simply because there was no time for this. He needed to focus on the task at hand. Besides, Roy was right. He wasn't floating around freely anymore. Roy was holding a tight grip on the ISS for both of them. He felt that this time that he could fire his weapon without flying away.

Throughout all the events from the last few minutes, he'd managed to maintain a death grip on the Desert Eagle. Glancing at the weapon, he was both surprised but also kind of proud of this fact.

One of the terrorists started firing. He fired only two shots at first, which seemed odd to Malote. Maybe they were just getting a feel for space, too, and were testing how to shoot in space. He could barely see his targets.

"Hey man! Give me some room. I can't see them.' Roy had been pressing down on him pretty hard. Roy responded by lifting up enough to give Malote a wide-open view of the terrorists.

Scoping out terrorists, he noticed they were struggling a bit to get a good grip on the weapons. One of them fired again, there seemed to be no recoil, and although the man did not move a single inch, his gun did flail momentarily. Malote, smiled, "Bad shots," he said as he took aim and opened fire again.

He fired only once. His shot was wide to the right, he adjusted his aim. He figured the bad guys were going through the same learning curve as himself. Apparently, no amount of training could prepare you for something like this.

He fired again. It took less than a second for the effect to be seen— he was pleased.

The visor of the terrorist coming up the truss was blown to bits. The glass fragments danced outwardly into the darkness as he flew backward. His body shot upwards, away from the station, before the tether recoiled him back down, slamming into the station. Lifeless, the body drifted up slowly and away. He swayed on the side of the station, about six feet into the air, unmoving.

Seeing his compatriot blown away prompted a rapid and violent response from the flanking terrorist. Although they couldn't see the shots, they could see the effects of the impact from what looked like automatic fire coming from this particular asshole. His aim was way off, and he had hit a couple of solar arrays shattering them nearby. "Turn me!! Turn me that way!" Screamed Malote while motioning wildly to his right. Roy did his best to spin them around to face a new threat. "Okay, Go!" Roy shouted back. Malote did his best to adjust his aim, but before he could fire, a bullet struck the space station less than three inches from their spot. "Shit, that was close."

Once again, taking careful aim, Malote fired back. This time his shot struck the terrorist on the left leg just below the knee. He lost his footing immediately but was holding on to his short tethers. Malote fired once again, this time striking the man square in the chest. The shot punctured the suit through and through expelling what looked like a fine mist of blood behind the mortally wounded combatant. "Yeah, that's right!" Malote yelled. "Come get some Putos! Okay, Who's next! C'mon!" Malote shouted. Scanning the ISS for additional targets.

"How many rounds does that thing hold?" Roy asked, trying not to break Malote's concentration.

"Nine in total. I still got five shots left! How's the refueling going?"

Roy glanced back to the gauge by the oxygen intake.

"Seventy-Seven Percent."

It was going relatively fast, but they still weren't done. Glancing at the two dead terrorists floating motionless, he caught sight of the third terrorist. By all accounts, he appeared to have changed his mind about attacking them, deciding instead, to crawl back towards where the Chandra had docked. This one wasn't following the Trusses and was just grabbing the handrails on the modules.

Not satisfied with leaving anyone alive, Malote took aim and fired. Roy was surprised by the shot and had almost let his grip go. Luckily he hadn't, but the motion had altered the shot's trajectory.

The shot missed slightly wide to the right. That is, it missed the terrorist. As they watched, the projectile hit the side of the Chandra. He knew it had hit because there was suddenly a small jet of liquid streaming out of the craft's hull. Roy suddenly shouted, Oh shit!".

Malote understood Roy's reaction to mean, "Oh Shit, you missed" and immediately retook aim and fired again. This time the round hit its mark. The third astronaut, who had almost reached his destination, flailed upward, motionless, except for floating away in the Chandra direction.

"Stop!" Roy shouted.

Malote, deeply satisfied with his performance, scanned the ISS one last time, as he declared. "Three shots left" For a moment, his eyes locked on some movement, and he almost fired at it, but it was not hostile. There was a module that was elevated slightly above the rest that was full of windows. Inside, Malote caught the excited expressions of some dude, he would have shot him, except this guy appeared very animated and... was he smiling? Yes, he was, cause he was now giving him a thumbs up. Malote paused for a moment and smiled to himself, knowing that he had a cheerleader. Even if he didn't know who it was, he felt as he did when Benicio would give him a pat on the back after a successful job.

"Jesus Man, that was violent," replied a horrified Roy. The astronaut hadn't meant it as a compliment, but Malote took it as one. "Thank you, vato, you didn't do so bad yourself."

Roy responded. "Just... Just save some rounds, just in case we need them later. Okay?"

Malote nodded. "Good point," he said. "Good thinking."

"Um, Thanks?"

Realizing that they were still in tandem, Malote complained. "Now get the fuck off me. This shit is weirding me out,"

"Yeah, okay, right, hold on a sec.," Roy immediately detached the carabiners. Malote looked over to the gauge next to the O2 line.

"Finish pompeandole la oxygen, puto!"

Roy, confused by the spanglish, understood, the words finish and oxygen. Surmising what Malote meant, he replied, "Yeah, Okay, i'll finish pumping the oxygen right away."

CHAPTER 17

Evacuation

Commander William Yelland impatiently watched as Karen was busily passing the multitude of small experiment containers and cases full of portable hard drives through MLM to the dock. He, in turn, was passing them on to the now docked Pegasus to Mike. They had formed a type of bucket brigade that Benicio had reluctantly joined to help move the cargo down past the crew compartment to the cargo hold. Dave had positioned himself down there and was strapping everything in as fast as he could. To Yelland, it looked like Dave was playing a game of Tetris as he positioned the cargo. Geo had ducked away quickly into the Cupola and was intently and excitedly looking outside. "Ooh, he got another one!" Geo exclaimed. "Guys, come look at this!"

This was probably the quietest gun battle in history. Sound doesn't travel in space, so the action taking place outside was lost on almost everyone but the participants. Inside the ISS, the only sounds they could hear were the scraping and clunking every Time someone made contact with the hull.

Karen floated over to join him, as she arrived, Geo exclaimed! "Jesus, That gangster guy just knee-capped this other one and—" "Oh my GOD!" yelled Karen! It seemed she didn't quite expect to see the violence outside. She really wasn't equipped to handle this kind of stuff. "He's killing them!" she shrieked.

Yelland had come up behind them. Concerned, he asked, "How's Roy? Is he okay?" Another banging sound was heard inside the station, somewhere far off. Yelland cringed.

"I can't see him too well, but I think he's okay. Look over there", Geo motioned, "Looks like he's joined in tandem with the other guy who's shooting."

Yelland, alarmed at what he was seeing, thought; *My God, Roy,* he thought. *What if he gets shot? What if I sent him out there to handle the oxygen transfer, and he ends up getting killed? That'll be my fault. That'll be...*

"Yelland?"

It was Karen, snapping her fingers in front of his face. "You okay? You zoned out. Stay with us."

"I'm not," he lied. "I'm just trying to process it all. I just can't believe that our survival depends on a couple of Sicarios."

A thin understanding smile crept onto her face but did not stay there for very long. There was yet another popping sound and then, a few seconds later, a much louder but distant hissing noise. This was almost immediately followed by a very light tremor, which was not so much heard as felt.

"Did we get hit?" Karen said, her eyes widened, terrified.

"I don't think so," a concerned Yelland said. "That...I think that's coming from the Chandra."

"Looks like it," Geo announced. "She just got hit. I think she's in trouble.."

"What kind of damage?" Yelland asked. "Can you see?"

"Not clearly, no. but I think I can see some kind of leak coming from her hull." Replied Geo.

Focusing his attention again towards the Pegasus, Yelland inquired through the comms, "Hey, Roy? Where are we on the O2 transfer?"

It took a moment to get a reply. When Roy's voice filled his earpiece, it was shaky and excited. "Eighty-three," he replied. "I'd guess another six or seven minutes, and they'll be full."

"Sounds good, Roy. We'll start getting r—"

"Hey, boss?" Geo interrupted.

"Yeah?"

Geo had left the Copula and had made his way into the MLM. He was staring at a display showing the layout of the station.

"We need to haul ass," Geo said. "Those terrorists have breached the node, and it looks like they have access to the Japanese research module and the Columbus Science Lab. It looks like they are trying to get into the Destiny module next."

"Crap. How long?"

"I closed and locked all the access points in the station between them and us, and it will take them some time to breach. I'm guessing, maybe... five minutes?"

With his nerves churning, he held his earpiece in place.

"Hey, Roy?"

"Yeah?"

"Any more terrorists up there?"

"No. Our new friend killed the three that were coming at us.

"You said six or seven minutes, right?"

"Yeah. Down to about five now."

"Okay. Look ...we've got terrorists on board. Looks like they're moving faster than we expected, so change of plan." Yelland was successfully adapting to this fluid situation. "When you're finished with the transfer, go ahead and get to the Pegasus, do not, I repeat, do not head back into the ISS. Acknowledge. Over?" He was reacting more to the ever-increasing tremor than anything else. "You got it. Acknowledged," came the reply.

Looking back at Geo and Karen, Yelland sighed. "Time to say goodbye to this station for now. We've got to get on board the Pegasus now."

Karen retorted, "What about the FSL? We can't let them have access to the SNOWCONE!" She was right. Yelland knew that there was no way they could let the bad guys near it. He nodded in agreement, "We'll figure it out, but we need to go for now."

"NO. We need to stop the terrorists before they get to it." She retorted.

"I understand that Karen, but we don't have any weapons. We're powerless against them. We NEED to get to the Pegasus and let them handle it." Yelland responded, realizing for the second Time exactly how dependent they were on these Sicarios. "It will take them some time to find the FSL. We'll stop them before that, but we need to get you to safety." Reluctantly agreeing, they headed towards the Pegasus. Geo was first, then Karen, and bringing up the rear was Yelland.

As they boarded the ship, Yelland looked back at the station. He could feel vibration getting stronger as he rested his hand on the passageway. He had a feeling that he would never see her again, and it kind of made him feel a tinge of sadness.

Just then, a random thought hit him that made him shudder. *Oof, I hope they don't take this out of my paycheck.*

CHAPTER 18

Introductions

Benicio was quite excited and entirely in his element as he watched the firefight happening outside the Pegasus. He was proud of Malote. Knowing they had a great payday coming, Benicio was quite happy to assist these astronauts in escaping the station.

Dave announced, "Roy and Malote just confirmed they've taken out three terrorists and have finished replenishing the O2. They're heading back to the airlock." Benicio had been helping Mike and Dave stow the experiment packages which were being transferred to the ship. They were working well together, but now there were going to be more people here. As he made his way past the pilot's chair, where Mike was sitting, towards the open dock at the tip of the ship where he could see inside the ISS.

He suddenly came face to face with Geo.

"Allo Mate" uttered a surprised Geo as he tried to read the stoic expression on Benicio. Trying to break the awkward moment, Geo spoke first. "I'm Geo from Sydney. I didn't get your name?" Benicio's face slowly unveiled a friendlier expression. "Benicio, from Brownsville, Texas." came the reply. Geo instantly smiled. "A Texan! You guys are crazy, mate, and I mean that in a good way", he said as he realized he had just called this gangster crazy. Benicio had found the accent somewhat comical. *Yeah, this guy is OK*, he thought. As he did, he shifted out of Geo's way to let him get on board. Looking down into the cabin, he could see that Dave had made his way back to his seat next to Mike, and now Geo was chatting with them.

Turning back to look into the ISS, he was suddenly face-to-face with a beautiful blonde looking back at him, their faces almost collided. "Oh," exclaimed Karen. "Hi, Who are you," she inquired. Surprised by the female presence, he instantly turned his game face on. "Hello, guerita. I'm Benicio, your very charming host. Welcome to the Pegasus." He charmed as he reached for her hand to help her board the craft. She smiled at this blatant and probably inappropriate introduction. She did, however, accept his hand and let him guide her into the vessel. As she passed him, he was checking out her backside. *Ay Mamacita*, he thought as he bit his lip.

"Can I help you?" Came a very unfriendly voice. Benicio turned around once again, only to be confronted by an angry face glaring back at him. Realizing he'd been caught checking out the attractive female, Benicio found himself feeling like a kid on prom night meeting his date's parents. Shaking the feeling off, he fell back to his standard angry response. "Who the fuck are you!" Benicio retorted as he regained his hostile demeanor. "I'm Commander Yelland. I'm in charge of this station", Benicio let out a quick laugh. "I hate to break it to you, but you ain't in charge of shit, vato, and we ain't on your station." Yelland's gut reaction was to grab this miscreant by the collar and teach him a lesson. As he did, Benicio produced a weapon seemingly out of nowhere and placed the barrel right under Yelland's chin. Surprised, Yelland instantly let go of Benicio's collar and just kind of froze in place.

"Hey! HEY! Guys, calm down. Benicio put that thing away before you kill us all" Came the sudden and desperate-sounding cry from Mike. Everyone in the cabin froze at the unexpected confrontation.

At that same moment, Roy and Malote's heads appeared from the cargo hold on the other end of the now crowded crew compartment. "What'd we miss?" Inquired a clueless Roy. Malote instantly recognized the situation. He and Benicio had been in this type of standoff too many times to count. Before he could stop himself, Malote instinctively called out, "Hey Boss!? Everything OK?"

Benicio, upon hearing his friend, snapped out of it. Pulling his gun away from Yelland, but without breaking eye contact. "We're good." He replied, although it wasn't clear whether he was talking to Malote or confirming with Yelland, Maybe both. Yelland nodded slowly and answered. "Yes, we're good," He continued his descent into the cabin, careful not to bump Benicio in the process.

A thin smile came over Benicio as he shook off the unpleasantness, and looked down towards Malote through the crowded compartment. He wasn't surprised to see that Malote was glowing like a kid on Christmas morning; he'd gotten to go outside and actually walk in space—*and* he'd gotten to take out some bad dudes, too. He was on cloud Nine.

Malote was pushing people aside as he made his way over to his buddy. Man, it was crowded in there. Geo and Roy were discussing the seating arrangements. Yelland and Karen talked to Mike and Dave about the FSL, telemetry, and other technical things. As far as he knew, they had done their job and were preparing to detach from the station to head home. That's when he realized that Yelland and Mike were looking more worried than usual as Karen was speaking. They kept glancing over to him and Malote. Floating down to them, he joined their conversation. "What? What is it?" he inquired.

"It's not good news. We're not done yet. We need you to stop the terrorists from reaching the FSL and gaining access to the Snowcone." Mike responded in all seriousness.

"The stupid snowcone, again?" retorted Benicio. As said the words, he recalled his conversation with the General and all that stuff about saving the world.

"Puta, Madre," he exclaimed. "Fine. A deal is a deal. Where's this Snowcone?"

"Hey, watch it!"

This cry came from behind them. It sounded like Dave. His voice was loud enough to catch everyone's attention. Turning around to see what was going on, when something slammed into Benicio's side. He wasn't sure what it was at first, but it knocked him back against the wall before he could see what was happening.

It was Tavo. He had come barreling forward, slamming into the gathered group like a bowling ball. He'd gotten free from his restraints somehow. Tavo slammed into the female astronaut. She went flying back towards the cargo hold, just missing it. Tavo was wildly shoving and pushing everyone in his way. Tavo bowled into Geo, knocking the astronaut back.

"Shit!" Roy yelled. "Who the fuck is that?" Completely unaware that the gangsters had brought their own hostage on board.

Malote was desperately making his way towards the out of control hostage. He nearly did it, too. But in the last moment, his foot got tangled on the tether still attached to him, and he suddenly stopped midair just an inch from Tavo's foot.

Benicio yelled, "stop him!" as he also lunged forward towards Tavo, who was now scrambling to go through the still open port into the ISS. "A Donde vas! Idiota!" Benicio screamed as he tried to follow.

Apparently not hearing him—or not caring—Yelland slapped the emergency close button that slammed the port shut in an inadequate attempt to keep Tavo from leaving. An angry Benicio punched the now locked door, screaming to whoever would listen. "Open it, open it! I've got to get that idiot back in here," Yelland responded, "I was trying to cut him off—!" Benicio was in his face right away. "What the hell do you think you're doing!" exclaimed Benicio. He gave a shove that sent Yelland sailing back to the far wall. Yelland, still not entirely understanding what had just transpired, replied. "Who was that?" as he held his hands up to stop the advancing gangster. "That's my fucking hostage, pendejo! Why'd you let him go! What the fuck were you thinking!" Benicio yelled. Geo and Roy came rushing towards him, in an attempt to stop escalating the confrontation any further.

"Hey! Cool it!" Roy said.

"Yeah, Boss, what's the deal? Let that asshole go. Who gives a shit." This came from Malote. Apparently, he had not yet figured out the severity of what just happened.

Benicio turned on his partner, furious that he seemed to be alone on this. It was rare that he was ever mad at Malote, but he felt the rage rising within him.

"Tavo! He just escaped!"

"So? We can get back home and..."

But Malote stopped there. Understanding dawned in his eyes, that understanding was quickly replaced by horror.

"Hijo de puta!"

"Exactly," Benicio said.

"Are we going to have a problem?" Roy inquired as he came between Yelland and Benicio.

"Depends," Benicio replied. Yelland interrupted, "I tried to stop him, but he got past the door before I could shut it." Benicio glared angrily at Yelland again as he continued to speak, "Look. I'm sorry about your friend, but he's not what's important right now. Terrorists are already onboard the ISS and seconds away from reaching the Snowcone. Your friend is as good as dead."

"I have to get him," Benicio stated with resolute authority.

"Our lives ain't worth shit if I don't get that puto back in here. I made a contract, and my life ain't worth shit if I don't deliver." he continued in a low, angry tone with a hint of desperation.

"The hell you do," Yelland said. "My priority is the Snowcone and the lives of my crew. Look, I'll show you how to get to the Snowcone. If you get rid of the terrorists, you'll probably save your guy." He then looked away from Benicio towards Mike, who was sitting at the controls of the ship. "Mike, how quickly can you get us out of here?"

"Wait, we're just going to leave that guy up here? That's a death sentence." Mike asked, a little confused.

"Not necessarily, I just need these guys to focus on getting the terrorists before they reach the Snowcone. Yes. It sucks, but these are the risks. The terrorists will likely kill him, and if we don't hurry, they'll take us hostage too. We can't let them have this win."

"Still," Dave said, slipping back into his seat next to Mike. "I understand what you're saying. I don't like it, but I get it. Look. We're all in Pegasus. We're good to go at a moment's notice. Hell, maybe we can save the station."

Yelland and even Benicio were taken aback by this statement. *Wait, were they really going to help him get Tavo back?* Benicio thought.

CHAPTER 19

Boarding

Amari wasn't quite sure why, but he was kind of disappointed in the lack of resistance. Making his way from the Chandra onto the ISS was utterly uneventful. Maybe he had worked it up too much in his mind; he had created expectations that were impossible to meet. He had a scenario wherein they would be in a glorious gun battle the moment the doors opened. But sadly, nobody was there to resist, and it irked and frustrated him a little bit. The place looked a little underwhelming.

Putting his weapon back into his holster as he looked around. He noticed that the station was also messier than he expected. There were computer cables everywhere. There were, what appeared to be, cushions or storage bags lining the walls and making the module he was in feel a lot more cramped than it should have been. Followed by Jarah, his expert technician, who immediately got to work on the locked node to give them access to the next node. Macchar had stayed on board the Chandra to keep the ship on standby.

Looking around, he checked his comms. "Report." He commanded. "Have you reached the other ship?" Expecting to hear from the men he had dropped off earlier on the exterior of the station.

"Sir, We're taking fire," came the desperate response. *What? Those damn Americans and their tactics. No way they could have expected them outside, much less prepared an attack.* Amari thought, alarmed at the unexpected news. "Well, fire back! Kill them! How many are there?" he desperately inquired. He heard a weird clanking sound not far from him from another part of the ship as he did so. "Sir, they've killed Amir! I'm headed around to flank them." came the exasperated response. "What! How many are there?" Amari repeated in a much more animated tone. After a few more seconds, another reply. "I can only see two. But only one is shooting back. They seem to be doing something to--" The transmission stopped cold as they heard more clunking from above. Amari hadn't heard anything but the part where only one guy was shooting back. "One guy!"

He yelled into the comms. "Take him out! Kill him now!" he shouted. Amari's thoughts wandered for a second. *What if all the stories were true? What if the American Military was as fierce and cunning as he had heard? He had always dismissed it as propaganda. But if they only sent one guy... and that guy had already taken out some of his men... maybe...* "No. No way." He scoffed at his thoughts. Just then another sound pierced the silence, this one was closer and sounded more like a pop. Suddenly there was a momentary shudder, and then vibrations as undefined sounds started coming from the Chandra. Amari could hear the low bellowing of metal warping from inside her. "Fuck this. I'm out of he—" Came to another transmission over his comms. "Respond!" Yelled Amari, "Someone Report! Anyone!" he was now angrily screaming into his comms. All he heard was static.

Macchar appeared at the dock as he exited the Chandra and quickly activated the emergency door. He turned to face Amari with a wild look in his eyes. Amari had not expected this sudden surprise, and the look on Macchar's face did nothing to comfort him. "What? What is it, Macchar? What happened?" He inquired.

Macchar, who was usually kept the coolest head in the room, was now turning paler than Amari had ever seen him. He was breathing hard. Something had gone terribly wrong to incite such a change in this man's demeanor.

Macchar, upon seeing his Boss's face, realized that he was unaware of the events that had just transpired. "I saw it!" He began to explain. "I saw it all." He was still breathing too hard to talk. He swallowed hard, trying to get himself back under control. After a few more breaths, he continued. "Our men were on point. They had split up and were attacking from three different directions. No way they could lose." but then...., he paused for a second. His unblinking eyes held a thousand-yard stare as he thought for a moment. "Then, I saw the American. He was lying underneath another American. He opened fire. I could see the muzzle flash from his weapon! I think it was a cannon! One-shot, Boom, our guy was dead. Second shot Boom He hit our other man in the leg, but then Boom! Blew him away through the chest! I saw his insides coming out his back! That's not normal! But then the last guy turned to come back when he shot again!" Macchar stopped again to catch his breath.

Amari, now thoroughly captivated by Macchar, grabbed him by the shoulders. "Then what? Tell me!" Amari needed to hear the whole tale. Macchar gathering his wits a little more continued. "The shot missed..." He took another breath. *Ah, ok, some good news, at last,* thought Amari. "But it hit the Chandra!" Macchar suddenly exclaimed, "Then he just blew away our last guy. He's floating away! They're all dead!". "Wait." Responded Amari, "What do you mean? They hit the Chandra?" Macchar's eyes grew wide again as he realized what that meant. "He hit the hull. It's compromised. I don't know what's going to happen, but it's a mess in there. I don't think we can use her to get away."

Amari quietly took in what Macchar had just told him. Shocked at how quickly they're plan had gone to shit.Just like that, his crew of six had been knocked down to three. *No matter*, he thought, *we're onboard the station. We can still carry out our mission.* Looking sternly at Macchar, Ansari said in a calm voice. "They did not die in vain. We will avenge their deaths. Now more than ever, we must complete our mission." Amari's calmer demeanor worked to help Macchar focus on the mission at hand.

"We're in!" an excited Jarah exclaimed. As he did so, the door leading to the module opened. "Yes!" shouted Amari as he floated into the module, only to come out a second later shouting. "You idiot! This is the Japanese Experiments Lab. We don't want to go here, it's a dead-end!" he shouted. "We need to get in there!" he said as he pointed to the other locked door adjacent to the one he'd just opened. "Oh. Sorry Boss!" He quickly replied. Instantly starting to work on the new door panel.

Amari held his head in his hands, his headache was coming back. *This is unbelievable, he* thought. *We're wasting precious time.* Well, the good news was that he still had Macchar at his side. He trusted this man more than anyone. And Jarah—an excellent fighter, extremely knowledgeable in all things electronic, and although a little spacey, he was still competent. They would do alright.

CHAPTER 20

Rescue Plan

Benicio was growing impatient. The more they talked, the less chance hc was going to be able to retrieve Tavo. That idiot had escaped into the ISS, and all these guys wanted to do was go home. And for some reason, it looked like Dave was coming to his defense. Honestly, he wanted to just go home too. But leaving Tavo up here was a death sentence not only for Tavo but for him and Malote when they got back. No. He couldn't leave him behind.

Malote was positioned next to him by the locked docking bay. Malote was trying to see if he could spot Tavo through the tiny porthole on that door. Benicio faced the now united crew below them as they argued about Tavo's fate.

"Basta!" Benicio shouted. As he did, he pulled out Malote's gun and waved it around, pausing it on Yelland. Immediately the compartment fell silent. The faces looking back at him had fear and anger in them. They looked almost offended that he had pulled his weapon on them.

"I'm not leaving him behind." he emphatically stated. As he did so, Malote also pulled out the large desert eagle and aimed it at them. Looking directly at Yelland, Benicio continued. "You are going to open this door. I'm going to go get Tavo, and you're not going anywhere until I get back. Do you understand me?" Benicio continued. "Malote, shoot anyone who tries to leave." Looking back at them. "Pinche Pendejos. You think you're all superior because you know all this space stuff. Have you no honor? We know that what we do is not legal, but we keep our word. We made a contract. Do you understand what that means? Our reputations and lives are on the line? I don't give two Shit's about this idiot, but I know that I HAVE to bring him back, and none of you will stop me.

His words seemed to have struck a chord with the crew. They looked flabbergasted at the accusations from this gangster street thugs had just accused them of not having any Honor. Yelland looked offended. Geo and Roy seemed to be Ok with this. They were comfortably safe on board the Pegasus and ready to go home. This was not their problem anymore.

Mike and Dave were speechless but nodding in agreement. They were sitting at the controls and could launch any second now. As everyone processed his impromptu outburst, Benicio motioned to Yelland. "Open it," he said.

Yelland was at a loss for words, simply nodded and pushed the button, opening the door. "Malote, don't let them leave until I get back, Ok, bro?" Benicio instructed him. "You got it. These vatos aren't going anywhere." Malote responded. "Hey, hurry back, ok?" sounding almost worried.

"No problem. I'll be right back", Benicio replied as he floated up through the now open docking port and into the ISS. Making his way through the MLM, Benicio realized that he didn't have a plan.

Oh shit, he thought. *Fuck it, I'll just wing it. It's what we're best at anyway,* he thought as he looked around, his eyes caught the large monitor showing the layout of the station. He could see that the blue-colored modules indicated that they were open, and the red ones were closed. Currently... If he was reading the information correctly, there was the Destiny module, and that little thing called... called the Cop...ula. Copula if he was reading that right. *What the fuck is a copula?* Well, he thought, *at least they labeled them.* Something else caught his eye. There were a few red-colored modules on the other end of the map. They were blinking pretty fast. What's *a pressurization alert? Hmm. That's probably what the vibration he was becoming aware of is coming from. Yeah, that's probably the bad guys.* He surmised.

Now, If I was Tavo, where would I go?

"Maybe you should check the cameras." came a voice from behind him. "What the fuck!" Benicio blurted out as he spun around as fast as he could. It was Yelland floating behind him. "Woah, there, relax," responded Yelland with his hands out. "Look," he continued... "What you said back there really got to me. I, too, am a man of my word. I'm here to help you." He paused for a second and then said in all seriousness. "I give you my word." he then motioned down towards the open dock. "Look." Malote was sticking his head out, and as he did, he shouted. "Boss, I think he can help. You should let him."

Knowing that Yelland knew how to work the controls of the station, Benicio relented. After all, the need to get Tavo back was more important than his desire to do things solo. Besides, this man seemed sincere when he gave him his word. Benicio made up his mind. "Ok. Ok. Your word is your bond. I accept. Now work this thing. See if you can find him", Benicio moved out of the way to give Yelland access to the station computer.

Yelland scanned through the cameras in all the modules. Some of them were disabled, and their screens simply read "No Signal." Suddenly, there on the camera to the Destiny module was Tavo. His hands were still bound, and it looked like he had gone to the furthest end of the module and was working to open the locked access door. "Found him," stated Yelland. "He's right around the corner. Looks like he made his way past this next node into the Destiny module right over there." As he said this, he pointed up to the node to which the Copula was attached. Above it was the locked doorway, which led to the Destiny. "Good," replied Benicio. "Let's go get him" as he started to head up.

"Wait! Look! Exclaimed Yelland, still staring at the screen. Benicio came back to see what had alarmed Yelland so much. There on the screen, they could see the interior of the Destiny Module. It was a long large white rectangular room lit by long white led panels along with two of the edges. On one side were laptops and displays. You could see what looked like a professional camera mounted on one end. In the far corner was Tavo. His hands were still bound, but he fiddled with the locking mechanism for the far side door, trying to access the node on the other side. "What's the problem, let's just go get him" Benicio stated. "No! Wait. Look!" replied Yellaned in a very concerned voice.

At that exact moment, the door opened, and they witnessed probably the worst-case scenario they could think of. The three intruders were standing there on the other side of the door. One of the men had grabbed Tavo, and it looked like either he was shaking him, or he was trying to fight them, but really he just looked like a fish flopping on a dock. "Shit," responded Benicio. "Shit, Shit.", confirmed Yelland.

"Shit. Shit. Shit." came from Malote. They glanced at him, still holding his position at the docking bay. "What?' He replied. "I heard you guys say it. It's got to be bad, right?" "Not now, Malote!" Whispered Benicio turning back to talk to Yelland. "Ok, they got him, what can we do?" Yelland thought for a second. Let's review. There are three of them, one hostage and two of us. Three if your friend joins us. They won't kill him, I think. They need a hostage." a quick laugh came from Malote. He whisper-shouted, "You haven't met Tavo. He's a moron. I'm sure they'll shoot him." "Not now!" Benicio whisper-shouted back.

Yelland, ignoring the exchange between the two, was trying to remember his air-force days, and all that training was coming back to him." Ok. I think I got it. We can execute an area ambush. But we'll have to wait for them to separate."

"What the hell are you talking about, let's just go in there guns blazing and take them out. Just.. well... try not to shoot Tavo," responded Benicio.

"Of course, that's what you'd do. "Yelland responded. He had seemed to have formulated a plan that he was getting enthused with." Trust me. This can work." He then proceeded to explain the battle tactic to Benicio. At long last, Benicio took a deep breath and said. "Are you sure this will work?" To which Yelland replied. "Honestly. I think it's the best plan we got."

Benicio turned to look at Malote. "Malote. Give him the gun." Benicio said. "What!" scoffed Malote, "I don't think so. You said we couldn't trust these people. Now you want me to give up my pistola! You've lost it. No way, man. No. Stas Loco." Benicio, obviously frustrated but not entirely surprised by Malote's answer, continued. "First of all, that's my gun. Second of all, I have this man's word of honor. and third.... well third." Benicio couldn't think of a third reason on the spot, but he settled on; Third, I'm the fucking Boss! Now give him the damn gun."

Malote recognized Benicio meant business. Not a time to fuck around kind of mood. He tossed the gun up through the zero-gravity towards them. Angrily he told them. "Here. But watch it, it only has three shots left" Yelland reached out and snatched the gun as it floated by him. Looking back down at Malote, he gave him a nod. "I'll give it back to you. I promise.". "You better, or else" Malote responded.

Yelland and Benicio both turned back to look at the screen. Benicio then said. "You tell me when."

Yelland nodded in agreement, his eyes not leaving the screen.

CHAPTER 21

Allah Provides

Amari floated quietly in the ISS entry hatch, watching impatiently as Jarah rewired the node. The thrill of having boarded the station with such little trouble was both exciting and worrying. Expecting something much more grandiose, the small space, coupled with all the exposed wiring and storage panels, was underwhelming. Turning his attention to Jarah, he wondered if the FSL containing the Snowcone would also be disappointing. No matter, Jara would open this hatch to the Destiny module soon. The Destiny housed the main communications array, where he would be transmitting his demands back to Earth. He wanted to make sure they broadcast as quickly as possible. The Snowcone could wait.

Glancing over his shoulder to the Japanese Lab, He watched as Macchar examined every console and panel as he searched for the Snowcone. It wasn't any of the areas they had already accessed. The man appeared overly paranoid that the combatants that had killed their men would surprise him from one of these other modules.

"Ah, Hah! I think I got it!" Exclaimed Jarah as he connected two wires. Amari watched the door. Nothing happened. The door didn't open. "Wait. Wait.", Jarah muttered to himself, "This one's more complicated than the last one."

Shaking his head, Amari admonished his Jarah, "We don't have time for this! Just get it open!"

Amari shouted to Macchar. "Macchar!"

"Yes, boss." Came the reply right next to his ear.

Macchar had silently floated back from the module and was quietly floating behind Amari. This had caught him by surprise.

"Don't do that!" he barked.

"Yes, Boss,"

"Stay close, we'll be heading into the Destiny module soon. I can't believe the space force took all our men out of here. We should have gotten here faster. No matter. Their likely plan is to evacuate the station, and I'm fine with that. Sadly though, we'll just have to execute our plan without any hostages." He lamented. "Damn! I really wanted a hostage", he muttered angrily to himself. "Jarah, how long now?"

"Not sure, maybe three min—" Mechanical sounds interrupted him, and the latch flew open. The trio of terrorists was now face-to-face with a very terrified Tavo. Eyes wide open, hands still bound together. Tavo screamed and tried to float backward, but to no avail as Macchar had reached out and grabbed him.

Amari smiled and let out a hearty laugh. "Allah provides," he said, pointing up. "Yes," replied a very smug Macchar as he restrained their new prisoner. "You wanted a hostage. Here's one". Amari looked the man over. What is this? This isn't an astronaut? Those clothes? That haircut? Why was he bound? Who the hell was this kid, and why was he here?

Assuming he wanted an interrogation, Macchar drew the lanky prisoner closer and grunted into a frightened face.

Tavo was spineless, and instantly started muttering away. "I don't know what's happening. I was on my way to the strip club, but these guys grabbed me and then the rocket I'm... in SPACE!" he was losing it. "Aahh. I just want to go..." he was really losing it. He continued, switching to Spanish, "Hay, no se qué locura está pasando pero, yo ya no quiero jugar." As he said this, he broke down crying. No one understood him. This sudden and unexpected outburst disgusted Maccha. He scowled and pushed Tavo away, still holding on to him.

Amari, who was used to dealing with professional soldiers, and hardened mercenaries, was, to say the least, disappointed. "Get a hold of yourself!" he barked at Tavo. "Have some self-respect, man." Amari leaned into his new prisoner with clenching teeth. "Now.....Tell me what I need to know." An evil smile came over him.

The man appeared to be an idiot but had given them all the information they needed. They knew that it was the Pegasus that had docked, and everyone was on board, ready to leave. Apparently, it had been hijacked by two Mexican cartel gangsters in south Texas. There were no Space Force on board. The man's name was Tavo and, if his story was to be believed, he was a hostage that had escaped. Tavo even gave Amari the Pin number to his bank account (Which nobody had asked for).

Tavo had offered to do anything he could to help Amari. Amari was not sure whether to believe the man or not—men would say all sorts of things to save their lives when it came down to it. But... It seemed that this coward was really too scared to be lying. He took him at face value.

"Ok!" Amari frustrated by Tavo's non-stop confession. "Shut up already!" Tavo continued talking. It was more mumbling now, but Amari had had enough. Amari motioned to Macchar, "Shut him up." Macchar produced some black duct tape from one of his pockets and immediately taped Tavo's mouth shut. Not just his mouth, Macchar wrapped the duct tape completely around his head a couple of times before ripping the roll-off. Tavo was not talking anymore.

"Thank you, Macchar," Amari smirked as he was relieved to have the silence back. Looking around the Destiny module, which they now had access to. Switching his stance from a hardened terrorist, now he was looking at the space more like a movie producer. Using his fingers, he formed a square to look through. He pretended to visualize the framing for the video they were going to send.

"Macchar. Where's the flag? Put it up. We need to make this look good." Macchar produced it from another pocket. "Right here boss, Where do you want it."

Amari responded, "Put it up back there against the door at the far end. It will make an excellent backdrop while still showing off the space. Don't you think?" The question was rhetorical, but Macchar knew what he meant. He unfolded the flag and put it up against the closed door. Amari, pleased with himself, inquired, "Jarah! How long till we can broadcast to the entire planet?". Five more minutes, I've just got to realign the dishes to the global broadcast—"

"Yes, yes, you're doing something technical." Amari interrupted, utterly uninterested in the how. "Just get it done!".

"Yes, Sir," an obedient Jarah replied as he turned his attention once again to one of the laptops.

Feeling pretty proud that his plan was coming together, he was reveling in his success. He wanted to show the world that they weren't safe from the Zalam Jihad, He would proudly display their flag and give his speech while standing next to a cowering hostage. He smiled as the thought of the glory he'd get from televising an execution from space. And that was just the first act, after that, once they controlled the Snowcone, his masterpiece would be complete. He'd launch it to the planet where it could do some real damage. He'd have his revenge.

Still...

Mexicans? He thought. He shook his head in disbelief. There was no way anyone could have planned for something so ridiculous. It almost made him wonder if it was a lie. No, it couldn't be, not with this little coward hostage he had. Tavo WAS the proof. No matter. No one could stop him now.

CHAPTER 22

Ambush

Having just been handed the Desert Eagle and tasked with a highly dangerous mission had Chris Yelland feeling ten years younger. Like he was back in the Air force. Sure, being an astronaut and running the space station was thrilling to be sure. However, they were facing some honest to God bad guys making this a different kind of excitement. Adrenaline surged through him as he examined the powerful weapon. What did that word mean that was etched into the barrel? 'MUERETE' must have something to do with Death, but what?

"Hey," he nudged Benicio.

"What?"

"What's this word mean? Muerete?"

Benicio sighed; he was focused on watching the array of monitors waiting for the right time to strike. He glanced at his familiar weapon and replied,

"Roughly it's a message to whoever you're pointing it to. More of a statement, really. The gun's purpose is to kill. So it says 'DIE.' It reminds me of how powerful a tool like this is. I don't ever use it lightly. Life and Death are both precious. I never want to forget it."

"Wow," replied Yelland, "That was deep. I wasn't expecting that from a..." Benicio raised an eyebrow as if to say, "Watch what you say next."

Yelland thought carefully, then continued. "I wasn't expecting that from a soldier." Benicio liked that answer. He gave Yelland a quick smirk and then turned his attention back to the screens. "Look!" Benicio pointed at the screen. "It looks like they're covering our door with a... is that a flag?"

"That's great," remarked Yelland, "it will give us precious seconds when we open the door. Now we just wait for them to be in the right positions, far from each other." He continued, "Now remember, I'll take the right side, you take a left. We want to take out these two guys before they can fire," he said while pointing at the figures on the screen. "This guy here is probably the one in charge. He might take a stand, but he'll likely run from the chaos, so he's the threat that can wait. Got it?" "Right," Benicio agreed. "No! You'll take a left. I'll "take a right Benicio rolled his eyes, "I got it. Like I said. Right".

"Oh," Yelland chuckled. "Oh, I thought you meant something else."

"C'mon man, Malote makes the jokes. Not you" He was just messing with Yelland at this point. It helped cut the tension.

"Ok, now what's the MOST important thing that we're NOT going to do?" demanded Yelland.

"Don't shoot the station." replied Benicio, "You've only said it about a thousand times. I got it."

"Good," said Yelland. Satisfied that his warning had stuck. "Ok, looks like they're moving into position. Let's get ready."

The duo swiveled the monitor to face the doorway so they could keep an eye on it from the node. They moved into position and were now crouching by the shut door, waiting for their moment. Yelland was ready to push the button that would automatically open it.

+++

Unaware of the impending ambush, the trio of terrorists was getting ready for their world broadcast premiere. Amari was excited, glancing at his notes just to make sure his speech would be perfect. "I'm going to stand here." He motioned to where he was already standing in the middle of the room. "We want to make sure the hostage looks much smaller, place him there, right next to, but behind me," Amari told Maccha. Maccha immediately grabbed their prisoner and floated him over behind and to the right of Amari. "Now. Maccha. You're going to have the honor of dispatching this soul from this world. You stand right over there on the far right until I give you the signal."

Hearing this, Tavo immediately reacted. He may not have been the sharpest tool in the shed, but he clearly understood that they intended to execute him on LIVE TV! He started trying to shout through the duct tape, but Maccha had made sure it was tight. He couldn't get a sound out. Ignoring him, Amari glanced over to Jarah, "How do we look? Are we framed correctly?" Trying to sound like an authority on TV broadcasting techniques. Jarah looked at his screen and gave them a thumbs up. "Showtime!" he shouted. "We're broadcasting in three, two," He didn't say 'One' because he'd seen enough movies to know you didn't do that. Amari, expecting the one, was confused. He gestured to Jarah questioningly? Jarah sighed and responded. "One. Go... You're live!"

This was his crowning moment. Knowing all eyes were on him, and his words would reverberate around the world really made his head swell. This was a remarkable moment. The moment he had lived for his entire life. He stared into the camera lens. ...and he went blank.

"Uh, Oh. Yes... As-salam Alaykum. Hello world, I am Miksa Amari, Commander of the Zalam Jihad. I have the pleasure of coming to you all from the great International Space Station". Altering his expression to a darker, more sinister appearance, he continued.

"This symbol of tyranny shall be no more under the jurisdiction of other nations. It belongs to the Zalam Jihad. This is the will of Allah!" so far, so good.

Basking in his perceived success. His expression shifted again. *Oh no, my speech, he thought.* His pride and the excitement of the moment has caused him to forget what he was planning on saying next. He looked down at the notes in his hand... He had lost his place. He was shuffling the cards in a desperate attempt to regain his momentum.

As he was busy trying to find his place, there was a distinct "clank" heard from behind the flag. Maccha, standing like a statue behind Tavo, heard it but tried to ignore the sound. He was maintaining his commanding pose as they were broadcasting live. Amari glanced at the flag for a second, but it hadn't moved, so he ignored it, going back to his papers.

There it was again, sounding like a muted pssssh. Was the door behind the flag opening? Ansari turned again; this time, he could see the flag fluttering. He *knew* the door was opening.

Before he could react, the flag came down as two figures flew through it. Yelland was headed straight for Maccha, his gun aimed right at his head. He screamed, "HOOAH!" At the top of his lungs! Maccha was a large man with quick reflexes. He instinctively grabbed the gun barrel before it could fire, but Yelland had already pulled the trigger. BOOM! came the large-caliber round flying through the air, as if in slow motion, it struck the side of the Destiny module, creating a golf ball-sized hole in the craft. "Oh shit!" Yelled Yelland as he came crashing into Maccha. Both of them flew into another wall as they battled for control of the gun.

Benicio had launched his way into the room, screaming, "AAAH LA PATADA PENDEJOS!" he carefully aimed at Jarah across the room, who was too surprised to move. The shot hit him square between the eyes, killing him instantly. His body just locked in its position except for the kinetic effect of the bullet knocking him backward. Benicio, still flying across the room like superman, passed Amari. The two men made eye contact. Amari, both surprised and furious, reached for his trusted Glock. He would have been able to shoot Benicio. Were it not for the sudden rush of wind as the air was rapidly flowing out through the hole Yelland had inadvertently added to the Destiny. The foot handles that kept Amari grounded in the Zero gravity environment had suddenly shifted. Knocked off balance and wasn't able to pull out the weapon in time. Benicio's trajectory had knocked him into the far corner of the Destiny. Disoriented, he was still ready to get back into the fight. Amari, knowing he was in trouble, quickly abandoned his position, grabbed Tavo, and used him as a body shield. He rushed past Benicio and out of the Destiny, propelling himself and his hostage back through another node.

Maccha was struggling hard with Yelland, and they were now spinning around, both men's hands on the weapon. BOOM! Another shot! This one zoomed past Benicio and hit the node's corner, causing a ricochet that shattered a nearby computer screen. Sparks were flying everywhere. The Destiny had been compromised. The strong gust of wind rushed through to the small puncture as their precious air made its way out to the cold vacuum of space. Maccha growled at Yelland, both of them locked in a fight for dominance. Yelland growled right back. His animal instincts were alive and well as they knocked against the wall opposite from the open hole.

Yelland thought *This guy is not going to beat me. I've got way more experience in this zero-gravity environment, and I know I can outmaneuver him.* This was the complete sentiment, but the idea that actually registered was. *Fuck this guy, I wanna live!*

At that moment, Yelland glanced over his shoulder, his eyes locked on the hull's threatening puncture. Instinctively and with all his might, he pushed Maccha off the wall using his legs as leverage, while at the same time spinning Maccha around. Slam! They hit the other wall— suddenly, there was silence. This surprised Yelland. Looking into Maccha's eyes, all he saw was shock. This man wasn't fighting back anymore. He was stuck, his body was covering the puncture. He was still reaching for Yelland but was being held in place by the forces acting on him. Yelland let out one last yell as his punch successfully connected with Maccha's jaw, knocking him out instantly. The module had, at least for the moment, stopped shaking.

Benicio floated over to Yelland; he looked at him and said. "Don't shoot the hull? That's what you said, right? It would be bad. Right? Now, look at what you did. You shot it twice!" Yelland accepted the criticism and replied. " Yeah I know, big mistake." I should practice what i preach."

Now it was Benicio's turn to take charge. "Yelland," he paused." You're done here." Benicio told him. "You've only got one more shot. I still don't have Tavo. I'll do this my way. Get back to the Pegasus. Tell Malote I'm right behind you."

Yelland just nodded. He was out of breath and out of responses.

"Good Luck," He said, "What are you going to do?"

"I don't know," Benicio responded. "But, I have to get Tavo back, no matter what."

CHAPTER 23

Last Stand

Benicio floated in silence as he watched Yelland head away from the Destiny back towards the Pegasus. He had found a new respect for this man. Yelland could hold his own in a fight, especially with such an imposing opponent. Benicio thought as he looked at the now unconscious Maccha stuck to the wall, his body keeping their precious air from leaving the station. The flag they had pulled down was floating down like a blanket coming to rest covering Maccha's face. He sighed for a second as he remembered that the battle wasn't over. He still needed to rescue Tavo.

Resolutely, Benicio focused his attention on the task at hand. Making his way stealthily through the node that his nemesis had escaped through. He peeked into the next module only to find that it was empty. *Huh*, he thought, *Where did they go*? As he entered this area, he noted that it was vibrating. The vibrations seemed to be coming from the Chandra which had been damaged in the earlier confrontation. Whatever had happened to her had caused her integrity to be compromised. Curiosity overcame him as he floated over to a small nearby porthole so he could see her hull. Lights were flickering, and she was definitely shuddering.

"Man, Malote really really knows how to mess sh—" POP! Broke the silence as a bullet flew past his head, missing him by an inch. The shot found its target in the node hitting a hydraulic line. Fluid poured out from some unseen mechanism.

"Ah la chingada!" Screamed Benicio as he pulled back against the wall. Looking around to find the shot's source, he realized it came from the next module labeled FSL. He hadn't seen who shot at him, but he knew this must be the place. "Don't Shoot!" Benicio yelled. "I just want to talk!" He was lying, but he needed to get a better view. "OK," came the response. "Show yourself! Hands first." Barked Amari, sounding a bit desperate.

There was no immediate response. But then, slowly, Benicio peered around the corner. He had tucked away his gun and immediately showed the man his empty hands. Looking around the lab, he could see Tavo, kneeling in the center of this mostly white room. Behind him was Amari, one hand on Tavo's hair, the other aiming a gun at Benicio. Behind him was what looked like a large round machine with many shiny cylinders meeting in the center. There were several control panels around its perimeter. The only reason Benicio took note of it was that it was the only thing in here that wasn't white or tied down.

Focusing on Amari, he saw a middle-aged man, eyes dark and empty. Benicio had seen eyes like that before, these were the eyes of an evil man. *No soul.* Benicio thought. As Benicio came into full view, both men sized each other up.

"So," the man finally replied. "You're the asshole that has so badly messed up my plans."

"Si Mon," Benicio replied. "Who the hell are you?"

Straightening out, as if to stand at attention, he replied, "I am Miksa Amari of the Zalam Jihad! I am on a righteous mission for Allah."

"I don't care about your mission. You have something that belongs to me, and I need it back." Benicio inched closer to the men in the room.

"Are you referring to this coward?" Ansari yanked Tavo's head back once again, pressing his weapon into his prisoner's head. "How can anyone want this... this.. dog!" He continued with disgust, although he was fully aware that Tavo was his only leverage.

"Yes," replied Benicio "I need him to come with me. He's necessary to me. Harming him won't do you any good. Just let me have him, and I'll walk away." He inched closer to the pair.

Amari thought for a second about Benicio's words.

"No," the man finally said in a petulant tone.

"I'd rather kill him," Amiri announced defiantly.

"Look," Explained Benicio as he inched closer, "Your men are gone. Your ride, as far as I can tell, is gone. You're not going anywhere. There's no one coming to help you." he paused for a second, "Estas jodido."

"I'm sorry I didn't catch that last part. What did you say?"

Suddenly, from behind Benicio, Malote popped out from around the corner, yelling, "He said your FUCKED, Puto!"

He came into view with the Desert Eagle in his hand. Amari, surprised, ducked out of the way. Time seemed to slow down. As Amari dove, the glistening filigree on the side of the deadly instrument caught his eyes. For a moment, his eyes focused on the word MUERETE, as if it was a prophecy coming true. "BOOM!" The last round shot across the lab, centimeters from Tavo's head, and found it's target hitting Amari on his upper chest throwing him back against the Snowcone. The smacking of his head resulted in Amari floating quietly, unconscious and dying.

A completely shocked Benicio looked back at Malote, looking at his buddy with a big grin on his face. Malote stated, "What? You didn't think I'd leave you all alone, fucker. We're compadres!"

A giant smile flashed across Benicio's face as he responded in kind. "Thanks, fucker. What took you so long. I almost had to shoot this asshole myself. Let's get the fuck out of this shithole. I'm done with space." Malote agreed. "Yeah, let's go home. I need a beer." They turned to go when Benicio remembered Tavo. "Oh shit! I almost forgot," He floated back to grab him. As he did, he removed the duct tape, quickly ripping it off.

"OOW!" Screamed Tavo.

"Ay, Ay, that didn't hurt." scolded Benicio, "Are you hurt? We need to get the fuck out of here?" Tavo, confused and angry, finally spoke. "Fuck you! I'm not fucking coward. I'll sh—"

A low guttural laugh interrupted Tavo. He turned his head slowly to find the source of the laughter. Benicio had frozen as the laughter caught him off-guard. As they looked towards Amari, he looked back at them through the tiny drops of blood that were weightlessly floating from his wound. What could the dying man before them have to laugh about? It wouldn't take them long to find out. As he slowly slanted to one side, their faces filled with alarm as they saw that his impact against the Snowcone had activated the orange button. Next to it, a small display showed a two-minute countdown timer had started. Amari was laughing, knowing that at the very least, he was going to set off the Snowcone.

Benicio shouted. "Orale! He turned on the Snowcone! Shit! Vamonos! Let's get the fuck out of here!" Tavo jumped forward faster than Benicio had ever seen someone jump. "Ahhh.." He screamed as he slammed into the node. Benicio shook his head while watching Tavo frantically panic. He thought I came back to rescue this idiot? "What a coward." He stated simply. Following the fool out of the lab, he turned his attention back to his friend, "Malote!" Benicio yelled. "We got less than two minutes before this whole place blows up! Get to our ship! MOVE!"

As the trio moved quickly through the station, the ISS seemed to shudder all around them. He could hear some sort of giant hissing noise, followed by what sounded like metal being twisted. Glancing behind him, he saw that the Chandra had now destabilized and was violently shuddering, threatening to rip the dock right off the station. "Oh Shit! We've got to MOVE!" He shouted urgently.

Malote shouted back, "The Pegasus is right there, just ahead!" They hurriedly made their way back through the modules. As he brought up the rear, Benicio paused for a second in the Destiny module and glanced around. The large combatant that Yelland had been fighting wasn't there anymore. He saw the flag was now stuffed in the small hole and was fluttering as it fought against the vacuum of space to keep the air from escaping. That's *weird*, he thought. *I wonder where that guy went? It doesn't matter, this place is gonna explode, and that will be the end of him.*

"Benicio! Hurry!" Malote shouted. He had already made his way into the MLM with Tavo.

"Right," Benicio responded, as he continued his way through the node back to the MLM. As they reached the dock, they could see Yelland looking at them from inside the Pegasus. He clapped his hands in triumph and gave a relieved little shout of victory. "I'm glad to see you guys, come on, get in here!" he said urgently as he gestured them forward. "The Chandra looks like she's going to tear away from the station, We've got to go!" Malote grabbed Tavo and shoved him down into the Pegasus. As he did so, he looked at Yelland, chuckled, and said, "If you think that's bad, the vato over there pressed some orange button on that Snowcone you guys keep talking about. We got about a minute before whatever that thing is goes off!"

"What!" Screamed Karen at the same time as Yelland as Malote passed him to get on the ship. She rushed to look out the porthole and yelled back. They've activated the eggshell! We've gotta leave! Yelland, still processing what she said, looked over to him. He wasn't expecting to get quite such an alarming response. Shrugging at Yelland, the commander responded, "Long story, I'll tell you later, but we gotta get out of here now!" Yelland looked back to Benicio with urgency in his eyes. "Ok, I hope that—"

He stopped here, confusion and horror in his eyes as he stared past Benicio. As his mouth opened to give a warning, Benicio turned around to see what was going on. His sudden movement rotated him a little too much; he nearly spun in a complete circle and might have actually done so if not for what happened next.

As he turned, he saw the giant soldier, the one missing from the Destiny emerging from the Copula. He had slouched over the side of the node into the MLM, clearly hurting—nearly dead from the looks of it, a trail of blood floating behind him as it left the wound on his back. But that did not stop him from firing his weapon.

His first shot went high and, thankfully, a little to the right. Benicio heard the impact over his left shoulder as he turned. The bullet slammed into the seal on the dock, busting some hydraulic line in it as fluid shot out. Benicio reached for his gun to retaliate against this new combatant, but his hand met emptiness, his weapon was missing! He looked down to see where it had gone, only to realize that Yelland beat him to it.

Yelland and the terrorist fired at the same time. The terrorist's final shot blasted a little left of Benicio. It tore into the airlock frame, causing a small explosion that shoved Benicio hard to the left.

Yelland fired two rounds from the gun he had swiped from Benicio. He let out a scream on the second one that was either the result of rage or disgust.

Both shots found targets. The first landed, just above the man's clavicle. The next one was a headshot that sent the man flying back with such force that it looked like a bull had kicked him.

"You okay?" Yelland asked as he let the gun float away from his hands.

"Yeah. I'm good." This was miraculously true. "Good shooting. Thank you."

"Yeah...just get in."

Benicio did so, gladly. He stepped through the dock and into the Pegasus. He saw that Malote and Roy were already in the process of securing Tavo to the same seat he'd occupied on the way up. The rest of the crew were looking at them as if not quite sure what to expect next.

"I heard shooting again," Geo announced.

"You okay?"

"Yeah, I just barely..."

"Hey, guys?" Yelland said, interrupting. There was fear and irritation in his voice.

"Yeah?" Geo asked, concerned about the seriousness in the tone of his commander.

Yelland slammed his hand against the dock in frustration and said: "So, we might... we might have a little problem up here."

CHAPTER 24

Oops

"What's going on?" Benicio asked.

Yelland was frantically trying to close the dock to the International Space Station. There was both fury and concern on his face as he frantically tried to shut the airlock. Behind him, the alarms sounded, the red lights flickering as the station's integrity was compromised.

"That last shot from that idiot up there tore right into the docking control. I can't close it."

"No response at all?" Mike asked.

"Zero."

"The alarms..." Roy said.

"Yeah. The whole place is going to either get sucked apart or blown to shit pretty soon. We need to get out of here as soon as possible. But we can't if I can't close this lock."

"Can you close it manually?" Benicio asked.

Yelland glanced at Roy and then with Geo then looked back at him. Slowly, he said: "Yes. But it has to be from the ISS side. And whoever closes it..."

There was an uncomfortable pause that made Benicio go cold. "Whoever closes it will be stuck there," he finished for Yelland. "Trapped."

"Yeah, that sums it up," Yelland said.

"I'll do it," Geo said at once.

"The hell you will," Yelland snapped. "You have two kids back home waiting on you. While we're at it, Karen isn't doing it, either. And Mike and Dave can't because they need to get us back home." There was a long uncomfortable silence followed by,

"Fuck it!" Malote blurted, surprising everyone. "I'll do it. Just show me what to do."

Yelland looked at Malote. "I don't know," he said. "You understand this is a death sentence, right?"

Malote, now resolute with his decision, responded, "Hey, I always wanted to be an astronaut like Lance Armstrong. Be pretty bitching to die in space in a blaze of glory, ain't that right, Benicio?"

"That's right, Malote. But...You can't do that to me."

"What do you mean?"

"You go home. You take Tavo and I'll—"

"That's a hard no to both of you," Yelland interrupted. "I respect the heroics, but I'm in charge of the ISS. I'll go down with the ship."

"Your mission went to hell because of us the moment we got here," Benicio said. "You married? Got kids?"

"Not currently married, but I do have a kid," Yelland nodded, a little wavering in his voice.

"Then get your ass on here and tell me how to close that airlock."

"No way," Malote spoke up again, a little angrier. "I'll do it, boss. I can—"

"We're not arguing about it," Benicio said. And oddly enough, he had a powerful sense of peace about it. He'd lived a mostly full life. He'd made many mistakes, sure, but he had come to terms with them all.

"Whoever's doing it, they've got to do it now," Roy said softly from the front, "We... We're running out of time. If the ISS is going to explode while we're still attached, then this is a moot conversation. We'll all go down with her."

"Benicio..." Malote said. He had never heard so much emotion in the man's voice.

"It's okay," Benicio said. "You go home and be the hero. I'll stay up here and live out your dreams...of being like Lance Armstrong."

"Lance?" Geo inquired.

"Not the time," Yelland said with a sad smile. Then, with a shrug of defeat, he motioned to Benicio and said, "Get over here."

Yelland walked Benicio through what to do. It was rather easy, actually. Though the control panel and functionality of the lock had been compromised, the manual mode was quite easy. It was the only way the door would respond. He and Yelland looked at one another with mutual respect as the ISS trembled around them. Somewhere from farther off, that strange creaking noise was getting louder.

"You're a fierce fighter and a brave one at that," Yelland said.

"Same to you."

The two men shook hands. Yelland looked back into the ISS one last time, a saddened look on his face. He then looked to Benicio and, with a thoughtful look, glanced back into the station.

"Look," he said. "You may still have a chance. It's a long shot because it's kinda busted. But after you close this latch, go back through the station and take a left then a right at the node. You'll see a door with the letters SC above it. That the Soyuz capsule. It's sort of like an escape pod. If you're lucky, Houston can control it remotely. It's not a guarantee, though; I mean, the station could be gone by the time they get the controls. I'll send the order in right away once the Pegasus is clear. If I were you, I'd give it a try. Even if it fails...well, the result will be the same. But it's at least a small chance..."

"Got it. Thanks. Now get in there. We're running out of time."

Something fractured and snapped behind them as if to remind them of this. A low rumble followed that Benicio could feel in his bones.

Yelland floated into the Pegasus and joined his crew. Quickly, Malote came to the doorway. "Take this," he said, holding out his hand to Benicio.

He was offering Benicio his medallion. He took it gratefully.

"She'll take care of you," Malote said.

Benicio smiled and said: "She has so far. See you in another life, my friend."

And with that, he tucked the medallion into his pocket and closed the door.

He saw that Malote had a tear in his eye as he slid the door shut. It was on rails like a door, only the mechanisms were hydraulic. Because those hydraulics weren't working, Benicio had to turn a large dial that slowly moved the door. He had to put some real strength into getting it to close. When he finally had it shut and resting securely in the frame, he pulled down the latch that sat at the top. This one came down a bit easier and snapped into place. It looked almost primitive, like Something you'd see on an old submarine, but he supposed it did the job.

Okay, he thought. *Now for that capsule. Maybe I'll get off this piece of shit station before it explodes or implodes, or whatever the hell it's going to do.*

He turned right away. As he did, he heard a slight commotion behind him as the Pegasus started detached from the airlock. Had he been a more sentimental man, Benicio may have gone to the copula to watch the Pegasus head back home. But he had never been one for sentimentality—especially not when his life was on the line.

Making his way back through the space station, he *was* overcome with the sudden realization that he was stranded in space. This was a mind-blowing revelation to him, as he thought that just a few hours ago, he was back home in Brownsville, hanging out by his truck. What the hell went wrong that caused him to be up here, now, alone.

The station shuddering and shaking around him forced him to put that all out of his mind. He needed to focus on the task at hand.

He passed the body of the dead guy that had nearly killed them in the end—the one that had blasted the dock, making it so that he had to stay behind. He gave the corpse a spiteful punch as he went gliding by him.

He headed further into the station, looking for the door to the Soyuz capsule. *Did he say a left then a right? Or was it a right then a left?* He thought. A moment later, there was another explosion. This one was smaller but seemed louder. It seemed to be coming from a bit further back, closer to the control center. The area he had just passed seemed to respond, as the walls began to shudder and crack.

This spurred him on even faster. He was going so fast that he almost missed the door he was looking for. He made himself stop by holding out his hand and pressing it against the wall. He could feel how unstable the station was as the tremors and quaking passed through him.

After a few panicky turns, he saw the sign, SC. At that moment, it was beautiful to him. It was much smaller than the airlocks he'd passed through, he would need to duck down a bit to go inside. He started for it, but that's when the station suddenly tilted.

He went forward, nearly falling directly into the capsule. Something else exploded behind him again. This time, almost right away, he felt an immense pressure coming from the station. He felt Something pulling at him, trying to pull him backward.

The vacuum, he thought, remembering how Yelland had explained it. He could also not forget how it had felt when Yellend shot through the hull, this was that same tremendous wind-like force that had nearly claimed them earlier.

It sent a jolt of terror through him, followed by a surge of adrenaline as if he needed more. Still, he did, he used every bit of his remaining strength to grab the hatch and pull himself. A bit of screaming, a string of curses, and he had entered the capsule. He shut the latch and did his best to figure out how to secure it shut. This was much different from the other mechanisms on the station. *Damn Russians*, he thought.

With that done, Benicio turned to face the tiny compartment of the capsule. It was cramped, to say the least. There were numerous bags and a laptop velcroed to the sides of the craft. A spacesuit and helmet was hanging above him, cables everywhere, and a cockpit seat in the center. There was an entire panel of buttons directly across from him, and he knew what none of them meant. *What the fuck is this? Russian?* "This is bullshit," he screamed. One of the buttons was lit and pulsating. As he studied the buttons, the capsule shuddered; Something else in the ISS had exploded. Through the closed capsule door, Benicio could now hear very alarming sounds of things banging and ripping through the station as it collapsed.

He still had no idea what to do next. He took the position in the seat and nestled in. He buckled himself up, always looking at the panel in front of him. As he looked, he saw two more small panels light up. The next explosion he felt was enormous. Even without seeing it, Benicio knew this was the one that would down the entire space station.

He didn't have time to worry about this, though. Immediately after the explosion, the Soyuz capsule was ejected from the ISS. It did not detach as it was designed to but was blasted off the ISS side like a bottle rocket.

Benicio barely had enough time to worry about what this could mean. Almost instantly, he felt the breath being pulled out of him and an immense weight coming down upon him. With a tremendous amount of G-forces pressing against him, Benicio passed out before he could even think to be scared out of his mind.

Everything went black.

CHAPTER 25

The Return

There was a deafening silence on the Pegasus as it sped through space rapidly descending back to Earth. Yelland looked around to see Dave and Mike at their stations, operating the ship. Tavo and Karen sat as comfortably as they could. Roy, Geo, and Malote were in jump seats, which had been cleverly hidden behind some panels but were now deployed. The only noise anyone made came in the form of a muted sort of muttering from Malote. He could hear every other word and knew that Malote was praying in Spanish.

They had all just watched the ISS explode. What remained was teetering out in space. As it had become nothing more than a considerable field of space debris. To the Pegasus pilots and Yelland and his crew, the destruction of the International Space Station meant that decades of scientific achievement had come to an end. While they all knew the world governments would get another into orbit soon enough, the station stood for greatness and was a light of hope for mankind. They all felt the loss.

As for Malote, Yelland knew he couldn't care less about any of that. The man had just lost his best friend.

Yelland was at odds with himself. A few hours ago, he'd been infuriated with Malote and Benicio. He'd loathed them almost as much as he hated the terrorists. However, those two civilians proved themselves to be quite useful if not downright heroic. He'd come to understand that while they would likely never see eye-to-eye on many things, Malote and Benicio were men of loyalty and, dare he say it, courage.

The Pegasus had reached the parking orbit and was waiting for the re-entry window to head back for Earth. Yelland got out of his seat and floated over to Malote. He leaned in close to the distraught man. "Benicio was a good man," he said. "From what I knew of him, anyway."

"Ha! That's how he fools everyone! He was a bastard! Ruthless and mean." Malote exclaimed." But he did have a heart the size of a mountain, and he always kept his word. That part sucks cause it hurts. You know?" He paused for a second and then gave Yelland an honest look. "I'm going to miss him."

"Whatever happens when we get back, I'll make sure everyone knows he died a hero."

"Gracias."

Yelland slowly floated up towards Dave and Mike. He glanced at Dave and then subtly pointed towards his ear. He then made a slashing motion across his throat.

Dave understood what he meant right away: *Kill the comms.* Dave pressed a single button that disconnected the communications between the crew. When Dave gave the nod, Yelland leaned in and whispered: "Anything from Houston?"

"They reported back and said they were able to connect to the Soyuz for a second, but then lost all contact."

"Any signs that he got in at all?"

"No, sir."

Yelland nodded. He'd been hoping for at least a glimmer of good news to pass on to Malote. But it didn't look like that was going to happen. The way he saw it, one of two things had happened. Either Benicio had gone down with the ISS, or he had managed to get into the capsule. Even if he'd made it to the capsule, the explosion had likely destroyed it as well. If not, Benicio would currently be hurtling through space without the ability to control the module.

Neither of these outcomes was good, but it did relieve Yelland a little bit that at least he wasn't the one in that predicament. Instantly he felt guilt for having thought that.

+++

Benicio opened his eyes and then quickly squeezed them shut as he had the mother of all headaches. Also, he was dizzier than he had ever been in his life. He was pretty sure his nose was bleeding, and he could feel that most of his muscles were sore. All this pain, although unfortunate, reassured him that he was still alive.

Groaning from the headache, he took stock of his situation. Sitting in the Soyuz capsule, he remembered being blasted away from the ISS like a bottle rocket as the station exploded. As far as he could tell, the capsule itself seemed to be unharmed. No alarms or flashing lights going off. The capsule seemed to be in one piece.

Looked out of the porthole in front of him, all he saw was black. He knew nothing about space, but it didn't take a trained astronaut to know that hurtling aimlessly through space was terrible news.

He had no idea how long he'd been passed out, and already, he felt the need to pass out overcoming him. Was he running out of air? He wasn't tired, not really, but he felt the need to close his eyes.

He fought against the sleep to look to the panel before him. Seeing what looked like a heavy-duty tablet, he reached for it. As he did, a single white light was flashing on the dashboard. He had no idea what it meant, but at least the capsule did have some power. Even if he did not know how to operate it, it was working. He suddenly thought that maybe those NASA folks were smart, and hopefully, they could figure out a way to fix it and maybe get him home. He did not hold too much stock in that idea. Hope was dangerous. But even if it came down to death, perhaps he could do that in comfort.

He gripped Malote's lucky talisman as he looked out into the darkness. There was nothing to see but an empty black void. He took the Santa Muerte figurine and let it float at the top of his small window to the universe. The small skeletal statue with her scythe seemed to be smiling at him. Was she mocking him, or perhaps she just knew they were about to meet in person.

He started to pass out. As he did, he thought he saw something outside, creeping into view through the veil of darkness. A small curved shape. Not Earth, but something else. Something grey and familiar.

His mind grasped for it, but he passed out before completing his thought.

CHAPTER 26

Boca Chica

The Pegasus touched down at the Space Logistics Launchpad in Boca Chica Beach, Texas. As he glanced out of the porthole, the first thing Malote thought when he saw the crowd outside with the flashes of lights was, *Oh Shit! It's the cops!* He knew that they had broken a lot of laws and thought it had finally caught up to him. Who knows how many law enforcement agencies had come to the Boca Chica Spaceport and were ready to haul his ass off to prison. Oddly enough, the one thing that clued him into what was really going on was Tavo. The idiot saw the commotion as they disembarked the Pegasus and had started to wave excitedly.

Malote slapped the moron's head, as he did so, he also began to understand their new situation. "Hey!" Tavo complained. "Dude, We're famous. Don't you get it? This is all for us!" Tavo said to Malote as he turned back to the crowd. *This wasn't law enforcement?* Malote thought. *No. This was a crowd of reporters. This was the press.*

He could see the reporters jabbering into their microphones to the cameras. He saw TV Vans with cameramen perched on top, trying to get a better shot and scurrying everywhere. As the flashes went off, all these people created a cacophony of noise as they asked questions over each other. Malote slowly smiled. It was awkward, to say the least, but he figured if he followed the astronauts lead, nobody would notice him. He was wrong, of course, Wearing his very loud Prada shirt, along with his large silver belt buckle, jeans, and boots. He stood out in stark contrast to the sleek white jumpsuits the astronauts were wearing. As he waved, he did notice that there *were* policemen and security out there, too. Still, they were so buried in the press and onlookers that they just blended into the sea of bodies.

Roy stepped up next to Malote and chuckled. "This isn't what you thought it would be like... coming back home from space. Getting all this attention."

"This is all for us?" Malote asked.

"Yeah, man. Soak it up. We're all heroes now. Benicio too."

"Nah. Benecio would have hated this." Malote responded, "He hated attention."

As they descended from the Pegasus, a few people came rushing through the crowd to meet them. Malote tensed up when he saw that four of them were military. The soldiers were flanking what looked like a general and another man—a skinny man that wore a simple black tee-shirt and jeans.

"Who's that?" Malote asked Roy as he motioned towards the man.

"That's Garrett Parker, He owns all of this. The Pegasus is his baby." Yelland answered unexpectedly as he joined their conversation.

Parker practically ran up onto the elevated walkway that connected the launchpad to the massive press area below. The crowd quieted down as Parker approached the crew. He eyed all seven people as they stood on the walkway; he was serious and expressionless as he did so.

Finally, his eyes settled on Malote. "So, you're the one..."

Malote felt a confrontation coming, "Yeah, Puto, I'm the one what?" Malote responded with his trademark hostility.

"You're the man of the hour." Parker suddenly broke the tension and smiled as he wrapped one arm around Malote and turned to face the crowd. Malote had not expected this response. Confused, he just looked at Parker, then at the crowd, and cautiously started waving while trying to put on his awkward smile. As they waved, Parker leaned in to speak to Malote's ear. "We've got a lot to talk about, you little prick. But out here, for right now, I need you to just smile and wave."

"Sir," Yelland interrupted Parker. "This man and his friend were responsible for stopping the terrorists and getting us out of there."

"Stop the terrorist? The ISS is gone. It looks to me like they won." Parker replied through his smile, trying to conceal his frustration.

"Yes, sir. But we only survived, thanks to these guys." Yelland replied as he waved to the press. Parker gave Yelland a quick stern but understanding glance. One of the soldiers handed Parker a microphone. He took a step forward and motioned with his hands for the press to quiet down. He took a moment, apparently putting his words together in his head, looked out across the crowd, and said.

"Ladies and gentlemen of the press. People of the world", He began. "Twenty four hours ago, we were reminded of the dangers that exist out in the world. A group of terrorists, with evil in their hearts, attacked the International Space Station, essentially attacked all peace-loving countries around the world." He paused for dramatic effect.

"We were shocked. That shock turned into anger, and that anger turned into an unstoppable call for justice. Determined to bring justice to these despots, we dispatched a special team from the United States Space Force" As he said this, he turned to one side to highlight the team behind him. Pausing for a second, as if to have noticed Benicio's outfit for the first time. "Ahem." Parker cleared his throat.

"This...unique...uh... team made up of Space Force, NASA, and of course Space Logistics Personnel.... and others."

He cleared his throat again,

"...without pause or concern for their own lives, raced to the International Space Station. Where they bravely delivered righteous retribution to those cowards while at the same time, saved our men and women from certain death!" There were cheers from the crowd... Parker continued. "Sadly, and although the International Space Station was a casualty in all of this, it's loss pales in comparison to the life we lost of one of our brave men.

He will always be remembered as a True Red White and Blue American Hero!" Applause broke out along with a deafening roar of approval from the press. As the cheering died down a bit, one of the reporters yelled out to Malote, "As an American hero, what do you want to do first?" he asked. Parker hesitated for a moment, then unsure what would happen next, handed the microphone to Malote.

Malote never in his wildest dreams had he thought he'd ever find himself in this position. Not having any idea what to say to this global audience, he took the microphone. Looking around at everybody for a few uncomfortable moments, he thought about his answer. Nodding confidently, he looked at the reporter and responded.

"I just want a Cerveza."

A stunned silence came over the entire complex. For a moment, all you could hear was far away seagull squawk. Just then, a burst of laughter and cheers came from the press. They loved his answer! Accepting their response, Malote, let out the biggest smile he'd ever shown and raised his hands in celebration! Yeah, he was going to be ok, and life from this moment on was gonna be great!

CHAPTER 27

Uta Madre! What now

Everything was grey: Grey and black. And there was a high-pitched ringing coming from everywhere.

Benicio blinked. *Was he dead? No? He was alive.* Somehow, he was alive. Some time between leaving the ISS and now, he must have hit his head pretty hard because as he looked around, he seemed to no longer be able to see any color.

Slowly, he sat up. He winced at the pain that cascaded through his body. He was pretty sure he had at least one broken rib and—

In sitting up, he realized that the Soyuz capsule was no longer moving. Not only that, but the windshield had a crack in it. He looked out past the crack in the window and saw what looked like a grey landscape. But it was weird, above it on the horizon was no sky, just more open black space.

Leaning forward, he placed his face against the glass. He scanned his surroundings. As he started to understand what had happened, his heart was filled with a strange combination of emotions, but mostly excitement, fear, and dread.

"The moon?" he said with a nervous chuckle which slowly turned into an outright laugh. "I'm on the fucking moon!" He yelled. Now he was laughing more like a lunatic.

It did indeed appear as if the Soyuz capsule had somehow been expelled from the explosion on the station with such force and against all the odds on the exact trajectory to catapult him to the moon. Where the Soyuz then crash-landed. He apparently "landed" inside a crater. He could see tall crater walls all around him, lining the crater as they curved up.

After Benicio took in the landscape around him, his attention moved back inside the craft at the panel in front of him. Nothing blinked or glowed. Apparently, the crash had knocked all power out of the capsule. He punched a few buttons, hoping for some sort of response, but there was nothing.

He glared out to the moonscape as he took stock of his situation. He had crash-landed on the moon, and the capsule seemed to be completely dead. He *at least* had a cracked rib, and there was a ringing in his ears that, thankfully, was starting to subside. He had no idea how much oxygen he had remaining, he had no food, and there was no hope of getting in touch with anyone on Earth.

He was going to die.

Damn, he thought. *I didn't expect this.* He had found courage on the Pegasus, sacrificing himself to allow the others to leave and live. He'd done this, knowing there was a good chance he'd die.

So mostly, everything was the same, but still, the moon? This was very different.

He took the Santa Muerte medallion out and kissed it. Thinking of Malote, he smiled to himself at the thought that he was on the moon... Just like Neil Armstrong—or, rather, Lance Armstrong. He laughed to himself, thinking *Stupid Malote. He would have loved this.*

He was here, on the moon; it would be a wasted opportunity if he did not get out of the capsule and go for a moonwalk. It couldn't be any more laborious moving around the International Space Station, he supposed.

Grimacing a little from the pain in his ribs, Benicio stuffed himself into the astronaut suit. As he put the helmet on, the lucky charm glistened in his eye. He grabbed it and wrapped it over the helmet, just like he'd done for Malote before his battle. He put on the gloves and, just in case... Now he didn't know if it was just habit, or instinct, but he grabbed his gun and shoved it into the utility belt. He turned towards the door and turned the dial that would open it. He nearly had it open, the effort causing his ribs to scream out in pain, but then the capsule started to vibrate then quake.

Shit, he thought. *Is this thing going to blow up just like the station?*

However, within seconds, he realized the tremors were not coining from the capsule. No...the shaking was coming from the ground—some sort of earthquake—or *moon*quake.

"What the hell?" he asked out loud, although there was nobody to ask. He was questioning his sanity. He'd never heard of earthquakes on the moon? Was there even such a thing he wondered?

He looked out of the mostly open hatch and watched as small clouds of lunar dust rose into the air as the surface of the moon shook. Then, slightly off to the left, his attention was drawn to something that once again caused him to experience some kind of emotion that was between awe and sheer terror.

The crater wall directly in front of him was moving—or at least that's how it seemed at first. But as a white light peeking out from behind the moving crater wall, Benicio realized that it was actually a door of some kind. *A hanger in the wall of a crater?* He thought. *Impossible*! And yet there it was, currently sliding open. It was a big sucker, too. It had to be at least a hundred feet tall, taking up most of the height along the crater wall. By the time it was fully open, Benicio could see that it was some kind of hangar door, maybe one hundred feet high and about three hundred feet wide. The white light that shone out of it lit up the crater floor.

The light began to dissipate as it was being blocked out by something emerging from that door. As it drew closer, Benicio could see a smooth curved silver shape. It did not touch the ground but instead hovered several feet above it. By the time it had left its hanger, Benicio knew what it was.

A spaceship. But nothing like the Pegasus or the Chandra. No...this was a UFO.

He watched with childlike fascination as the disc-shaped craft came to a stop in front of him. Then, from behind it, emerged several much smaller shapes. They looked humanoid, but given what he knew about UFO's, Benicio doubted they were human.

He grinned despite himself. He was glad to have sacrificed himself for his friend, but Malote would most definitely have *loved* this.

The spaceship stopped moving, hovering over the ground about thirty yards away from the capsule. The little figures were headed in his direction. As they stepped closer, he was able to get a better look at them. They did not look exactly like the little green men he had heard so many stories about, although there was a close resemblance. These guys had shiny silver space suits with clear domes for helmets. He could see their faces. They had featureless grey skin and, while they did have the fabled huge almond-shaped eyes, they curved back slightly, almost like an insect.

Instinctively, Benicio checked his weapon. His Desert Eagle was likely back on the Pegasus, back in Texas by now, he supposed. However, the Malote's pistol still had nine rounds that were aching to be used. He then reached for the capsule door, grabbed the handle, and pulled it completely open. He stepped out onto the moonscape, where the approaching aliens were closing in fast.

"Hola Muchachos!" he shouted as he grinned ear to ear. "Who wants to dance?"

The precious Santa Muerte medallion around his neck shimmered for a second as if to bless its owner. It glistened in the sunlight.

To be continued...

Anthony Acosta Sc.D. lives in McAllen Texas with his wife, Fabiola, and Daughter Kennedy.

He's an Aspie and a Geek and has a deep passion for all things Science Fiction.

He's a huge fan of the works of Isaac Asimov and Douglas Adams.

Anthony Acosta is an Author and former Lecturer. Learning to code when he was 12 years old on a Commodore Vic 20. He's been creating, running, and managing computer networks and telecommunications projects since the 80s.

He holds several advanced degrees in computer science and has been instrumental in the development of many internet technologies. Anthony has 25 years as a computer professional, including 17 years as an IT professional.

Working as an independent consultant for PR firms on a wide variety of emerging technology projects as well as being the creative force behind many general market marketing campaigns. He is adept at conceptualizing, developing, and executing all aspects of digital and traditional marketing.